DIARY OF A DUMMY

GOOSEBUMPS®
MOST WANTED

#1 PLANET OF THE LAWN GNOMES

#2 SON OF SLAPPY

#3 HOW I MET MY MONSTER

#4 FRANKENSTEIN'S DOG

#5 DR. MANIAC WILL SEE YOU NOW

#6 CREATURE TEACHER: THE FINAL EXAM

#7 A NIGHTMARE ON CLOWN STREET

#8 NIGHT OF THE PUPPET PEOPLE

#9 HERE COMES THE SHAGGEDY

#10 THE LIZARD OF OZ

SPECIAL EDITION #1 ZOMBIE HALLOWEEN

SPECIAL EDITION #2 THE 12 SCREAMS OF CHRISTMAS

SPECIAL EDITION #3 TRICK OR TRAP

SPECIAL EDITION #4 THE HAUNTER

GOOSEBUMPS®
SLAPPYWORLD

#1 SLAPPY BIRTHDAY TO YOU

#2 ATTACK OF THE JACK!

#3 I AM SLAPPY'S EVIL TWIN

#4 PLEASE DO NOT FEED THE WEIRDO

#5 ESCAPE FROM SHUDDER MANSION

#6 THE GHOST OF SLAPPY

#7 IT'S ALIVE! IT'S ALIVE!

#8 THE DUMMY MEETS THE MUMMY!

#9 REVENGE OF THE INVISIBLE BOY

GOOSEBUMPS®

Also available as ebooks

NIGHT OF THE LIVING DUMMY
DEEP TROUBLE
MONSTER BLOOD
THE HAUNTED MASK
ONE DAY AT HORRORLAND
THE CURSE OF THE MUMMY'S TOMB
BE CAREFUL WHAT YOU WISH FOR
SAY CHEESE AND DIE!
THE HORROR AT CAMP JELLYJAM
HOW I GOT MY SHRUNKEN HEAD
THE WEREWOLF OF FEVER SWAMP
A NIGHT IN TERROR TOWER
WELCOME TO DEAD HOUSE
WELCOME TO CAMP NIGHTMARE
GHOST BEACH
THE SCARECROW WALKS AT MIDNIGHT
YOU CAN'T SCARE ME!
RETURN OF THE MUMMY
REVENGE OF THE LAWN GNOMES
PHANTOM OF THE AUDITORIUM
VAMPIRE BREATH
STAY OUT OF THE BASEMENT
A SHOCKER ON SHOCK STREET
LET'S GET INVISIBLE!
NIGHT OF THE LIVING DUMMY 2
NIGHT OF THE LIVING DUMMY 3
THE ABOMINABLE SNOWMAN OF PASADENA
THE BLOB THAT ATE EVERYONE
THE GHOST NEXT DOOR
THE HAUNTED CAR
ATTACK OF THE GRAVEYARD GHOULS
PLEASE DON'T FEED THE VAMPIRE
THE HEADLESS GHOST
THE HAUNTED MASK 2
BRIDE OF THE LIVING DUMMY
ATTACK OF THE JACK-O'-LANTERNS

ALSO AVAILABLE:
IT CAME FROM OHIO!: MY LIFE AS A WRITER by R.L. Stine

DIARY OF A DUMMY

R.L. STINE

SCHOLASTIC INC.

Goosebumps book series created by Parachute Press, Inc.
Copyright © 2020 by Scholastic Inc.

ISBN 978-1-338-35573-4

10 9 8 7 6 5 4 3 2   20 21 22 23 24

Printed in the U.S.A.   40
First printing 2020

SLAPPY HERE, EVERYONE.

Welcome to *SlappyWorld*.

Yes, it's Slappy's world—you're only screaming in it! Hahaha!

I'm in a good mood today. That's because I looked in a mirror! My reflection is almost as good-looking as I am!

I know this book is going to be *awesome*. That's because it's about ME! Hahaha!

I'm so brilliant, I'm the only one on earth who can outsmart myself!

Do you know how smart I am? Of *course* you don't! How *could* you? Hahaha!

I have powers, too. I can control people. Watch. I'm going to make you read the next sentence.

THE NEXT SENTENCE.

See how I did that?

Our story today is about my diary. Why do I keep a diary? I like to read books about fabulous characters. And I *love* sharing my brilliant thoughts—with myself! Haha!

1

The fun begins when a boy named Billy McGee and his sister, Maggie, find my diary. And when I say *fun*, of course I mean scream-out-loud scares!

I call this story *Diary of a Dummy*.

Go ahead and start screaming. It's another one of my frightening tales from *SlappyWorld*.

1

You're probably asking, "Hey, Billy McGee, how did you get to be the new kid in this fancy middle school? And with a hole in your sneaker, and wearing your cousin Shawn's ragtag old jersey with the stain on the front that won't come out?"

I know you're saying, "Look at those guys you're playing soccer with. Check out their designer jeans and NBA sneakers. Check out their cool haircuts. Bet their dads didn't cut their hair in the bathroom with an old pair of scissors."

Go ahead and make comments. I know I look a little different from them. Maybe my dad doesn't give the best haircut in the world.

But, you know, we're just trying to save up some money. And everyone has been really nice to me since I started here at Middlebury Middle School last week. (We call it Middle Middle.)

The kids I've met don't care if I wear the newest sneakers or if my red hair is long and wild. Or if my cousin's old clothes are a few sizes too big for me. (My dad says I'll grow into them.)

But when you're in the middle of sixth grade and you move to a new school, you feel like an outsider no matter what. I mean, these guys here on the soccer field with me have known each other forever.

My sister, Maggie, and I are the only new students in Middlebury this year, and we don't know anybody. But we're making friends.

"Hey, look out!" I tried to kick the ball to Damien, who's on my team. But my foot slid right over the ball and I flew headfirst to the grass.

"Unnnnh." I heard everyone laughing as the breath whooshed out of my body.

"Glad you think it's funny," I choked out.

Damien helped me to my feet. "Billy, have you ever played this game before?" he asked.

That gave everyone another laugh.

"We didn't have grass at my old school," I said. "We were tough. We played on dirt."

"That explains it," the kid named Ramone said. I'm pretty sure he was being sarcastic.

We started the game again. It went okay till I misjudged a kick, and the ball went sailing off the field, across the street.

"Don't know my own strength," I said, trying to cover up my embarrassment.

Damien patted me on the back. "Bet you're good at other sports," he said.

4

"Not really," I confessed.

See? These guys are really nice. No one seems to care that I don't exactly fit in here.

So how did Maggie and I get to Middlebury?

Well, it's kind of a long story.

Here's the short version. My mom died and my dad lost his job. We couldn't afford our house. It was big, and it came with big bills. The three of us were miserable and depressed.

Someone told my dad about a fixer-upper house here in Middlebury. A "fixer-upper" means a falling-down wreck. And so we really had no choice. We moved. As soon as Dad saves up some money, he'll start fixing it.

Maggie is in fourth grade, and she's a lot better with new people than I am. I mean, she's not shy at all. She's funny and fun and very peppy, and kids always like her right away.

It takes me a little longer. I haven't been sleeping well, and I think a lot about Mom. But as I said, the kids here have been okay.

I glanced down the street.

Oh no.

My stomach tightened with dread.

Cold dread. It's the one thing I'd been worried about since I started here.

And it was coming toward us fast. And it was going to pass right by our soccer field.

And I knew there was nothing I could do about it.

I took off running, kicked the ball to Ramone, and shouted, "Let's go! Go!"

I was hoping to keep them from seeing what was rolling down the street. But no way.

They were all staring along with me as the bright red-and-blue truck, pulling a huge blue trash dumpster, rolled by the soccer field. And they all read the tall yellow words painted on the truck door: DUMPSTER DAVE.

And then . . . yes . . . yes . . . no way to stop it . . . no way to keep it from everyone. My dad was at the wheel of the truck. Everyone watched him stop at the curb, the dumpster squealing behind him. And they all saw him wave to me.

"Hey, Billy, how's it going?" Dad shouted.

And then my new friends all knew. Dumpster Dave was my dad.

My dad took a job hauling trash to the Middlebury town dump. The job was one of the reasons we moved here.

6

I knew my face was bright red as I waved back to Dad. I shouldn't have been embarrassed. I knew I shouldn't have. But I was.

The dumpster squealed again as Dad started the truck up and pulled away from the curb. The guys watched it rumble away. Then they all turned to me.

"Your dad is Dumpster Dave?" Damien asked.

I nodded. I tried to make a joke. "The job really *stinks*."

They all laughed, but it was kind of phony laughing.

Damien had a twisted grin on his face. He jabbed me in the belly with his fist. "You know what *that* means?" he asked.

"No. What?"

"It means you're Dumpster Billy."

That wasn't funny at all. But everyone laughed like it was the best joke ever. And then a few guys kept repeating it. "Dumpster Billy. Dumpster Billy."

Well, I can survive this, I thought.

I didn't know just how bad things were going to get.

"This school is so seriously cool," Maggie gushed. "We all get tablets so we can play *Fortnite*."

Some parents probably wouldn't know what *Fortnite* is, but of course Dad does. Ever since Mom died, he's tried really hard to keep up with "what the kids are doing." He means well. "Maggie, why do you play *Fortnite* in class?" he asked.

"It's a special project. To see how much about the real world you can learn while fighting zombies," she replied.

Dad spun the wheel and turned the truck onto Manchester Road. Maggie and I were jammed in the front seat beside him. He glanced at me by the window. "And how was *your* day?"

"Okay," I said. I sure wasn't going to tell him the guys called me Dumpster Billy. He would feel terrible.

The sun had lowered behind the trees, and everything appeared gray. Dad clicked on the headlights. The dashboard clock read 7:05.

"Sorry it's so late," Dad said, squealing to a stop as the light above the road blinked from yellow to red. "We'll grab some dinner after I dump this load off."

"How come you're so late?" Maggie demanded. She had a small pack of Skittles in her lap. She was eating them one by one, and she wasn't sharing.

"Save me one," I said, grabbing for the pack.

She smacked my hand away. "No, Billy. You'll spoil your dinner!" She cackled, pleased with herself.

I'm used to her.

"I'm late because I had an extra-large haul today. But I'm not going to let this job get me down in the dumps," Dad said.

It was a lame joke. But of course Maggie and I laughed.

Dad has a long, narrow, bloodhound-type of face. He always looks serious, even when he's being funny. He has black hair cut very short, with a little bald spot on the back of his head. And he keeps complaining about the dark circles around his eyes. But he's always had those.

The sky had deepened to purple. The trees on both sides of the road stood like shadows, black against the dusky sky.

Dad eased the truck through the entrance to the dump. We bumped over the rocky ground,

9

the loaded dumpster squeaking and creaking behind us.

The dirt road ended in a circle. Dad followed it slowly, then threw the gear into reverse and backed the dumpster toward the shallow ravine where the trash was piled.

Peering out the open truck window as we edged backward, I could see an ocean of trash. Chairs and cartons and big plastic garbage bags in all shapes, some standing upright like living creatures; shimmering metal objects; tall heaps of stuff I couldn't recognize; stacks of news-papers; piles of clothing.

A strong breeze blew and made everything move. The trash was tinkling, shifting, crinkling, and rattling. *It looks alive,* I thought. I shud-dered and realized my heart was pounding. Why was I letting my imagination go wild like that?

Dad pulled a lever on the dashboard, and I could hear the dumpster start to move behind us. I shoved open the truck door and jumped down to the ground. Maggie followed me.

We watched the dumpster slowly tilt up, ready to spill its load onto the pile of rubbish in front of us. The dumpster squealed as it moved. The trash began to slide out, crashing onto the ocean of garbage that seemed to stretch forever.

"Can we explore?" Maggie asked.

Dad rubbed his chin. "Sure. But don't go too

far. It's dark. Some of the stuff in here could be dangerous."

Dangerous?

If only Maggie and I had listened.

Dad turned back to the dumpster. Maggie and I walked along the edge of the trash. A bright half moon hung low in the sky. It sent an eerie gray light over everything. Somewhere far in the distance, a cat cried.

A shiver ran down my back.

"All this garbage is freaking me out," I said. My voice came out muffled by the creaks and groans of the shifting trash.

Maggie turned and stepped into the ravine of rubble.

"Hey—where are you going?" I called.

In the distance, the cat let out a long, mournful howl.

Maggie took several steps, her shoes crunching on plastic garbage bags. Then she bent down and lifted something from the pile. "Billy, look. Someone threw away an old PlayStation. The controllers are here and everything."

"Put it down, Maggie," I said. "It's probably broken."

Of course, we were desperate to have video games. But that wasn't in the budget. Maggie and I didn't even have phones. I'd bet just about every kid at Middle Middle had one.

She dropped it back into the tangles of trash. "Come here. There's lots of cool stuff," she called.

So I followed her, stepping carefully over squishy bags and boxes and heaps of old clothing. And that's when we found the suitcase.

I saw it first. A very large brown suitcase. The moonlight made the metal latches glow. I pointed. "Maggie, check it out. It's like new."

She turned and stood across from me. "Think there's anything in it?"

"Only one way to find out." I grabbed the handle and stood the suitcase up. I gripped the latches and flipped them up.

The lid fell open.

"Oh—!"

I stumbled back as a creature came leaping out.

A blur of pink and gray. It happened so fast, I couldn't see it. The animal landed on my sneaker with a heavy *thump*.

"Oh . . ." I struggled to tell Maggie. "On my foot! On my foot!"

The creature slithered under my jeans. Warm fur brushed my leg. I could feel scratchy nails prickling my skin. My whole body shook.

"Help me!" I cried. "It—it's climbing up my leg!"

"Billy—" Maggie's eyes were wide with horror. "What . . . what is that?"

4

"I—I think it's a MOLE or something!" I tried to scream, but it came out in a choked whisper.

I shook my leg hard. I kicked at the air.

Too big to be a mouse or a rat. It pressed against my skin. I leaned back and kicked with all my strength.

The big creature slid out from under my jeans leg and went sailing over the trash. I watched it land hard on its feet. A mole. Yes, it was a fat mole.

It scampered away in a straight line. Suddenly, three or four other moles poked up from the carpet of junk and went running after it.

I took a deep breath. Tried to step out of the trash. Tripped over something I didn't see. And flopped onto my back.

"Maggie—help me!"

I felt something sticky on the side of my neck. I tried to hold my breath against the putrid stench. Why wasn't Maggie helping me to my feet?

Still afraid to breathe, I pulled myself shakily to my feet. Maggie had the suitcase lid raised and was peering into the case. "Billy, look. There's something else in the suitcase."

I gasped. "Another mole?" I could still feel the prickly feet digging into my leg.

I hurried over to my sister. "I had a mole climbing on my leg, and then I fell into the trash," I said. "Don't you even care?"

"You should be more careful," she said.

"Ha. Funny."

I peered into the case. Two round black eyes stared up at me. Round eyes in a wooden head. The face had an ugly grin painted across it.

"It's a dummy," Maggie said. "You know. Like ventriloquists use."

The thing was folded into the case. It was dressed in a gray suit with a white shirt and a red bow tie. Its black hair was painted on its head. It had a small chip broken off its pointy nose.

"Why would someone throw a perfectly good dummy in the trash?" Maggie said.

I reached in and lifted it out of the case. It was heavier than I thought it would be. The grinning head tilted to one side. At the end of its dangling legs were black shoes, scuffed and stained.

14

"Maybe the ventriloquist decided to retire," I said. "Or maybe a doll collector threw it away. Or a puppet-maker who couldn't sell it."

The dummy appeared to stare at me with its wide-open eyes. The grin appeared to grow bigger, but I knew I was imagining that.

"I think he's cool," Maggie said. "You know, people find treasures in the trash all the time. That's what Dad says."

I slid the dummy back into the suitcase, and we carried it to the truck to show to Dad. He was fiddling with the dumpster, but he turned when we came near.

"I wondered where you were," he said, mopping sweat off his forehead with the back of his hand. "I told you not to wander off."

"Look what we found," I said. I pulled open the suitcase lid and lifted the dummy out.

"Can we keep him?" Maggie asked.

Dad squinted at the grinning dummy. "Better put him back," he said. "He's probably crawling with bugs."

"No, he isn't," Maggie said. "He's clean."

I decided not to tell Dad about the mole that jumped out of the suitcase.

"We'll check him out when we get home," I said. "He's totally cool. Let us keep him, Dad."

"Please. Please." Maggie went into full begging mode.

15

Dad sighed. "Okay. Okay. Put him back in the case. Maybe we'll spray him before we take him inside."

We both cheered and thanked Dad.

Of course, we were making the biggest mistake of our lives.

5

By the time we washed up and changed our clothes, we were starving. Dad threw some frozen dinners into the microwave. The chicken dinner is pretty good. But the macaroni and cheese dinner is always too soft and too runny. We always fight over who has to eat that one.

While we waited in the kitchen, I lifted the dummy out of the suitcase to study it. My cousin Ariel had a dummy that she got for a birthday present. She used to try to do a funny ventriloquist act with it, but she wasn't very funny.

Ariel's dummy had an opening in its back. You put your hand inside it, and you could control the dummy's mouth and eyes.

I pulled up this dummy's coat jacket and searched all along his back. But I couldn't find an opening.

In the jacket pocket, I found a small slip of white paper, folded in two. I unfolded it and read the words in tiny type.

17

"Hey, this paper says the dummy's name is Slappy," I told Maggie.

She snickered. "Dumb name," she muttered.

I squinted at the slip of paper. "Weird," I murmured. "There are a bunch of strange words here. I don't know what language they're in."

"Read them," Maggie said.

I read the words out loud: *"Karru Marri Odonna Loma Molonu Karrano."*

"Hey!" I cried out. "The dummy just blinked!"

"The eyes are meant to open and close, Billy," Dad said. He slipped an oven glove over his hand to take out the microwave dinners. "See how the eyelids slide up and down?"

"I could swear—" I started.

"Get that thing out of here," Dad said. "We haven't had a chance to clean him yet. Put him in the back room while we eat."

I stuffed Slappy into the suitcase and carried him to the little storage room by the back door. Then I returned to the kitchen, my stomach growling.

"Let's all wash our hands one more time," Dad said. "I worry about the bacteria at the dump."

So we went and washed our hands again. I soaped myself all the way up my arms. I wondered if I still smelled like the trash heap.

When I got back to the kitchen, Dad and Maggie were staring at the table. I turned to see what they were looking at. My mouth dropped open when I saw Slappy sitting up in a chair at the head of the table.

"I asked you to put him away," Dad said.

"But . . . I *did*!" I stammered.

"Is this your idea of a joke?" Dad said. "I told you, that dummy is probably infested."

"*YOU'RE the one who's infested!*" the dummy shouted. "*Infested with STUPIDITY! Hahaha!*"

I gasped. Maggie clapped her hands to the sides of her face.

"It *talks*?" Dad said. "That's impossible!"

"*Your brain is impossible!*" Slappy rasped. "*Impossible to FIND! Haha!*"

All three of us just stared at him, unable to speak. I had this sudden feeling that I was dreaming and about to wake up.

"*Is this what you call DINNER?*" the dummy yelled. "*It smells like something I STEPPED in!*"

Slappy tossed his head back and laughed.

Dad's face turned red, and he gritted his teeth. That's what he does when he gets angry but doesn't want to shout. "Get that thing back in the suitcase—now!" he said.

"*YOU go in the suitcase!*" Slappy cried. "*And take a long trip. Don't let the door hit you on the way out! Hahaha!*"

"How is he doing that?" Maggie said. "How is he talking and moving on his own?"

"I don't care," Dad said, his jaw clenched tight. "Just get him out of here. We'll figure it out after dinner."

"Aww, can I have one more chance, Pops!" the dummy rasped. *"Let me give you a present. A nice dessert."*

Slappy leaned over the table and opened his mouth wide.

"Oh noooo," I moaned as I watched a fat brown cockroach climb out of his mouth. The cockroach dropped onto the table and scampered under a dinner plate.

Then another cockroach poked out between the dummy's wooden lips and fell onto the table. Then another. And another.

We all gasped and moaned as a *stream* of fat cockroaches poured onto the table. They swarmed over our plates, in our food, and across the table.

Slappy tossed his head back again and spit a few of the disgusting bugs across the room.

"Stop it!" I screamed. "Stop it!"

The dummy turned and belched a stream of cockroaches at me. They clung to my T-shirt and began to swarm up my neck. Cockroaches prickled my cheeks.

"Stop it! Stop!" I didn't want to touch them, but I had no choice. I slapped one off my face. Then I twisted and squirmed and tried to pull them off the front of my shirt.

I kept swatting at them, screaming the whole

time. Or was that Maggie screaming as she watched in horror?

"Hold still!" Dad tried to help brush them off, but Slappy just spewed some more. He sent a spray of cockroaches into my hair. Then his shoulders heaved up and down as he giggled.

"Hate to be a pest." He laughed, really enjoying himself. *"But I just love BUGGING people!"*

Slappy's laughter rang in my ears.

Dad dove forward and raised both hands, ready to grab the dummy around the neck. But Slappy ducked to one side. Dad lost his balance. With a loud groan, he hit the floor.

Slappy laughed his ugly laugh. Then he turned to Dad, who was still down on the floor. *"Would you BELIEVE it?"* Slappy screamed. *"You were right! I AM infested! Hahaha!"*

Maggie and I struggled to wipe the disgusting roaches off my clothes. Dad jumped up and lunged for the dummy. But Slappy dodged away again— and Dad went sailing into the broom closet door.

The door sprung open. Dad steadied himself against the wall.

I uttered a startled gasp as Slappy suddenly turned in his chair—and leaped into my arms. "Hey—!" I managed to cry out. "I—I've *got* him, Dad!"

"Who has WHO?" Slappy rasped. He spun his

head around and dug his hard wooden lips into my earlobe.

"OWWWWWW!" I howled as the pain shot over my whole head. I grabbed my ear. It felt wet. Was it bleeding?

"Hey—what's eating you, kid?" Slappy cried. *"Is it ME? Haha!"*

Giggling, the dummy jumped to the floor. *"Let's all calm down, folks!"* he shouted, waving both hands over his head to get us quiet. *"It's been fun. But we have to get serious."*

Cockroaches scuttled down the table legs and swarmed across the floor.

I thought I had brushed them all off me until I felt a tickle—and pulled one out from behind my ear.

"Let's talk about how you three are going to be my SERVANTS for the rest of your lives!" Slappy shouted. *"You'll be obeying my every wish— FOREVER!"*

His head turned from Dad to Maggie, then to me. *"I can see you're not too smart. But do you GET it?"*

"No way—" I started to protest.

But I saw Dad raise his hands, as if in surrender. "Okay, Slappy," he said. "We know we can't fight you. We give in." Dad stared down at the dummy, his hands still raised. "We'll be your servants. How can we serve you?"

7

"Dad—!" Maggie cried. "What are you *doing*? Are you giving up so quickly?" She had tears in her eyes.

But I knew what Dad was up to.

I knew he was stalling for time. I knew Dad had a plan because his eyes kept darting to the open broom closet. I figured he was waiting for the right moment to use something from the closet to bring Slappy down.

"I'm sorry, Maggie. But we have no choice," Dad told her. "Slappy has powers. We can't fight him."

"Very smart, Pops," Slappy said. *"You're a wimp and a loser. And you know when to give up!"*

My brain was spinning. I wanted to help Dad. But how?

I decided maybe I could distract the dummy to give Dad time to get to the broom closet. I curled both hands into tight fists.

"Maybe Dad is ready to give up," I said. "But *I'm* not!"

I raised my fists and charged at Slappy.

I only got two steps.

The dummy raised his wooden hand, waved it once in the air—and I froze.

I mean, I really froze. My muscles all tightened. I was totally stuck.

I strained and struggled, but my arms wouldn't budge. My hands were locked into tight fists. And my legs . . . my legs were as solid and heavy as stone.

"Can't move . . ." I choked out in a faint whisper. "Help me. I . . . can't . . . move."

"Slappy—let him go!" Maggie screamed. "Unfreeze him! Let Billy MOVE!"

The painted grin on the dummy's face appeared to grow wider. *"Want to hear a secret?"* he said softly. *"I don't know HOW to unfreeze people. I only know how to freeze them."*

I struggled to breathe. My stomach wouldn't move in or out. Every breath I took hurt all the way down.

I felt an itch on the back of my neck. A cockroach? I couldn't move my hands. I couldn't scratch it away. It prickled my skin. I felt myself start to sweat.

I couldn't blink, but my eyes moved a little from side to side. I saw Dad edge toward the broom closet against the wall.

"Let him go! Unfreeze him!" Maggie cried again.

"Maybe someday I'll learn how!" Slappy exclaimed. *"Hahahaha!"*

Maggie's face turned red. "You can't DO this, Slappy!"

The dummy laughed again. *"I already did it! Your brother is a good-looking statue. Would you like to join him?"*

Slappy raised his hand to freeze my sister. And that's when Dad made his move. He snatched a broom from the broom closet and rushed at Slappy from behind.

He swung the broom hard at the dummy's head. So hard that Slappy went flying from the chair. He sailed a few feet in the air, then came down hard.

His wooden head hit the floor with a loud *smaaaack*. His arms and legs were spread out flat.

"I think he's dead!" Maggie cheered happily.

I felt a burst of energy. My knees bent, and I staggered a few steps. I turned my head from side to side. I tested my hands.

"Hey—I can move again!" I cried. "That broke the spell. I can move!"

"Yaaaay!" Maggie shouted. Then we heard a moan and stared at the floor.

"Oh no," Maggie cried. "He's not dead!"

With a groan, Slappy pulled his legs together and started to sit up.

Dad grabbed a metal bucket from the closet and slammed it down over the dummy's head. Slappy groaned again. *That's NOT on my bucket list! You're giving me a HEADACHE!"*

"Quick—get him back in the suitcase!" Dad ordered.

I tossed the bucket aside and grabbed Slappy by the head. I lifted him off the floor. Maggie had the suitcase open by the kitchen door. I gripped the dummy tightly and strode toward her.

Slappy kicked both legs hard and whipped his

arms, trying to twist free. His head slipped from my hands. But I caught the shoulders of his suit jacket before he fell.

"*You'll pay for this! You'll pay!*" the dummy screamed. "*Let me go, servants! I'm warning you. You'll be EATING cockroaches before I'm through with—*"

He didn't have a chance to finish his sentence. Dad and I jammed him into the open suitcase. Maggie gripped the lid tight to make sure it stayed open. Something fell out of the case. But there was no time to see what it was.

I grabbed Slappy's legs and tried to fold them over his head.

But the dummy had a surprise for me. As I leaned over the case, struggling with his legs, his hands shot up. They grabbed me by the shoulders.

I cried out in pain as his wooden fingers dug into my skin. Dad tried to yank me free—but the dummy had astounding strength.

"Whoooooaaaa!" I wailed in horror and shock as I realized the dummy had tugged himself up.

Slappy stood—and swung me down hard. My head hit the suitcase lid. Bright red and yellow lights flashed in my eyes. I didn't move for a few seconds. But it was long enough for Slappy to accomplish what he wanted.

I saw Dad make a grab for me. Too late. The

dummy jammed me into the suitcase, tucked me in tight, and slammed the lid shut.

I heard the latches click.

I was breathing so hard my chest throbbed. I strained against the lid, pressing my head against it, trying to force it open.

I stopped when outside the case, I heard Slappy shout at my dad: *"Okay, Pops. Let's take this trash to the dump!"*

What happened next?

I don't know.

I couldn't see a thing. I was locked in the suit-case. It grew hot in there very quickly, and I started gasping for breath. The air was running out fast.

Over the steady beats of my pounding heart, I could hear voices in the kitchen. Shouts and angry cries.

I held my breath, trying to slow my panic. But my heart kept pounding away. My face was drenched with sweat. I was folded up tight, my muscles all aching.

I tried to bump the lid open with one shoulder. But there was no way I could move enough.

Outside the suitcase, I heard a struggle. A crash. A loud thud.

I heard Maggie scream, "Nooooo!"

I heard Dad utter a hoarse cry.

Then another crash.

My heart pounding so hard it hurt, I heard Slappy's cackling laughter. And then the laughter cut off suddenly with a sharp cry.

Then silence.

The longest silence of my life.

What did Slappy do?

What did Slappy do to them?

Did he really hurt them? Did he knock them out?

What is he going to do to ME now?

10

When the suitcase lid popped open, I screamed.

Someone unfolded my legs, and now I could see. The light pouring in blinded me at first. Blinking hard, I struggled to move my arms.

Dad lifted me from the case.

"Dad—" I choked out. "Oh wow. Oh wow. You're okay?"

Dad nodded.

"Slappy? Where is he?" I demanded.

Dad tried to help me stand, but my legs started to give way. I caught myself before I fell.

I saw the dummy sprawled on the floor, not moving. "Wh-what did you do to him?" I stammered.

"Maggie used a frying pan on him," Dad said. "Let's just say if his head wasn't made of wood, he'd have a terrific headache." Dad was breathing hard, his chest heaving up and down. "Hurry—get the dummy into the case."

He held it open while Maggie and I jammed the

evil thing in, folded him, and twisted him. Slappy didn't attempt to move. He was totally out.

Dad slammed the lid shut and latched it. A few minutes later, we were in the truck, on our way to the dump.

We didn't talk for a long while. I stared through the window at the passing trees, black against a dark sky. The moon had slipped behind the clouds. It was pretty late, and we were the only ones on the road.

Maggie broke the silence as we neared the dump. "I feel like we're in a horror movie! I keep expecting the dummy to come roaring up from the suitcase and attack us."

"I think we'll be okay now," Dad said, eyes staring straight ahead through the windshield. "Craziest thing I ever saw," he muttered. "We can't tell anyone about this. No one would believe it."

Dad parked the truck at the edge of the dump. He grabbed a flashlight, clicked it on, and handed it to me. "So dark tonight. Keep this at our feet, Billy."

He carried the suitcase in both hands. We followed him across the ocean of trash. We walked slowly, carefully toward the far end.

Dad set the case down. "I think this is far enough. No one ever comes over here."

I held my breath. The smell here was pretty gross. Squinting into the tiny beam of light, I saw a family of raccoons in a circle, pawing into a large trash bag.

"Cover the suitcase up," Dad said. "We don't want anyone to find it."

Maggie and I grabbed trash bags and piled them on top of the case. Maggie found a stack of decaying clothes, and she spread them on top of the trash bags.

"Completely buried," I said. "I think we're safe now."

"I think *everyone* in town is safe," Dad agreed. "I don't know how a wooden dummy can come to life. But I think the dummy's story is over once and for all."

We drove home with the radio cranked up. Singing along. Feeling happy and relieved.

At home, we celebrated with some dishes of ice cream. The cockroaches had all disappeared into the cracks of the floorboards. Dad fretted that he couldn't afford to call an exterminator, but we knew they'd return when the lights were out.

"Too late to do homework," I said, spooning up the last of my Rocky Road. "Dad, can you give us a note to our teachers saying we couldn't do homework because we had to fight a living dummy?"

"Sure thing," Dad said. "No problem." We laughed. He went to the basement to see if he had any cans of cockroach spray.

And that's when we found the book.

Actually, Maggie spotted it first. A small square book with a dark brown cover. She lifted it off the floor.

"That fell out of the suitcase," I said. I hurried over to examine it with her.

"It's a diary," Maggie said. "I wonder who it belongs to?"

SLAPPY HERE, EVERYONE.

Who does it belong to? It's mine, you dummies. We wouldn't have a very good story if it wasn't mine—*would* we? Hahaha.

It's so good, I can't put it down. It's my favorite book. The main character is so interesting and lovable. And it has such an awesome plot—MY LIFE! Hahaha.

And now Billy and Maggie are enjoying the diary. Believe me, it will lead them to a very exciting adventure.

Spoiler alert: This story has a happy ending.

A happy ending for ME!

Deal with it! Hahahahaha.

11

We carried the little book to the living room. The front cover read: *My Diary by Slappy.* We plopped down in the middle of the couch and started to thumb through it. The pages were lined and gray and silver-tipped. Pretty fancy.

The diary was written in blue ink. The handwriting was small and neat.

"It all looks totally normal," I said. "Like anyone's diary. Except it was written by a dummy."

"This is awesome!" Maggie exclaimed. "Do you think it's worth a lot of money?"

I shook my head. "A dummy's diary? Who would want it?"

"Scientists, maybe?" Maggie replied.

"I don't think so." I shrugged. "I bet no one would believe that a dummy wrote it."

We both thought about money a lot. We wanted to get our house fixed up. We were desperate to help Dad. But I knew that finding this diary wasn't exactly like winning the lottery.

"Let's start at the beginning," I said, flipping to the front of the book. "Maybe we can find out something about him—like how a dummy can be alive. That might be worth some money."

We hunched close together, raised the diary close to our faces, and started to read:

Dear Diary,

I am so glad to have you in my hands. No one understands me. Only *you* understand me, Dear Diary. Only you know the real me.

You know that I'm not evil. I would hate for people to think I am evil. I am just *mischievous*.

I like to have fun. I like to play jokes on people. I love to laugh. Laughter is what keeps me going when times get tough.

I don't want to be hated. I want people to like me.

I want people to like me—so they will be happy servants and do everything I tell them to! Hahaha.

"That sounds like Slappy," I said, rolling my eyes. "He floods our house with cockroaches, and then he says he wants to be liked."

Maggie elbowed me in the ribs. "Keep reading."

I have so many wonderful memories to tell you about, Diary. Where shall I start? At the very first birthday party I went to?

Dean "The Dream" Harrigan was my ventriloquist. Yes, Dean thought he controlled me. It took him a while to see that I was in charge.

Dean "The Dream" had big dreams. He wanted to be a famous ventriloquist. He wanted to entertain kids all over the world.

He started out small, at birthday parties. Moms and dads hired Dean to put on a funny show for their little four- and five-year-olds. And guess who was the real star?

Slappy "The Nightmare"! Hahahaha.

I love kids, Dear Diary. I love them fried with mashed potatoes on the side. Or roasted over a low fire. I even like them *boiled*! Hahaha.

And I especially like them when they become my servants for life!

So there I was, my first birthday party. Sitting on Dean Harrigan's lap. The kids all perched on the floor in front of us. Donny, the big, blond, red-cheeked birthday boy, in the front row, waiting for his birthday treat.

And what an amazing treat I had for Donny. I gave it my all!

I threw up on the kids in the front row. Of course, I saved a special hurl for the birthday boy!

Then, while everyone was screaming and

carrying on, I jumped off Dean's lap and ran headfirst into the birthday cake.

What smashing fun. The cake exploded. You should have seen it, Dear Diary. It flew in all directions. Cake all over me. Cake splashed onto the wallpaper. A huge mountain of cake on the carpet. Ha.

I guess that's when kids started crying.

Or was it when I sank my choppers into Donny's hand and nearly bit it off? Donny squealed like a little pig. Haha.

I love to surprise people, Diary. It gives me such a thrill to get people excited.

It was a great party. I still remember the look on the father's face as he struggled to pry my teeth off his son's wrist.

And, of course, I'll never forget Dean "The Dream" Harrigan. How he just stood there, eyes bulging, mouth hanging open to the floor. Hey, it wasn't my fault Dean was arrested. I'm not the one who called the cops.

Donny's parents called the cops. And— boo-hoo—Dean "The Dream" never worked another kids' birthday party.

And ta-daa! A good time was had by all.

At least, by ME!

I raised my eyes from the page and turned to Maggie. "Slappy is *horrible!*" I said. "He's totally evil."

Maggie twisted a strand of her red hair between two fingers. "He's *sick*. And he doesn't know it. He thinks what he did was *funny*."

I turned the page. "Look at this. He's bragging about how he burned someone's house down."

I turned a few more pages and started to read again:

Dear Diary,

Jillian Jones and I had fun at the school talent show. At least, I had some fun.

Jillian found me in my suitcase in an alley and brought me home. She begged her parents to let her keep me. And they finally said yes.

Jillian wanted to do a ventriloquist act with me at the big talent show her school has every year. The show is at night, and they invite the parents to come to the auditorium to watch.

Jillian wrote a lot of jokes for me to say. She practiced with me every night in her room after she finished her homework. She really wanted to be a hit.

In the act that she wrote, I was a bad boy who never did his homework and never did what my parents asked me to do. She tried to teach me manners and how to be good, and I kept messing up.

It was pretty funny, Diary.

But guess what? When we got onstage, yours truly made it a *lot* funnier!

The night of the talent show, Jillian was shaking with nerves. She was seriously stressed out. I wanted to tell her to relax, that I'd take care of everything.

But she thought I was just a dummy. And I didn't want to spoil my surprise.

The show started. The auditorium was jammed with parents and kids. All of Jillian's friends came to cheer her on.

With me under one arm, Jillian paced back and forth backstage as act after act went up to perform. Lots of cheers and applause. She seemed to get more nervous by the minute.

Finally, her turn came. She stepped onstage into the spotlight and sat down on a folding chair. She propped me carefully on her lap.

"Hello, everyone—!" she started.

And that's when I went into action.

I waved one hand and froze her. Yes, Diary, I froze her like a stone statue and turned her mind blank.

She sat there in silence, and everyone in the audience stared at her, waiting for her to start her act.

The auditorium grew very silent. And Jillian was silent.

Such lovely quiet, Diary. You could almost *hear* the silence!

I grinned at everyone and watched them wait. And wait. And wait.

Then people started to mumble and stir. I could hear whispered questions. *What's wrong with Jillian?*

Finally, Ms. Haskins, the principal, walked onstage. She was biting her bottom lip, and her eyes were narrowed. I could see she was worried about Jillian. She crossed the stage and stepped up to Stone Statue Jillian.

"Are you okay?" Ms. Haskins asked.

That's when I waved my hand again and *unfroze* Jillian.

She blinked and stared up at the principal. "Uh . . ."

"Just a little stage fright!" I made her say. *"No worries."*

Ms. Haskins nodded. Then she turned and walked back offstage.

Jillian shifted me on her lap. She looked very confused. She squinted out at the audience. "Now, Slappy—" she started.

That's when I waved my hand and froze her again.

Hahaha.

Yes, I'm laughing, Dear Diary. What a wonderful joke. Is anyone as clever as I am? I don't think so.

The audience gave Jillian a few seconds. Then everyone began talking at once.

I heard her mother and father shouting: "You can do it, Jillian! Go, Jillian! Go, Jillian!"

Of course, Jillian was under my spell. She couldn't move.

Finally, Ms. Haskins returned to walk Jillian off the stage. "Come with me," she said. "You'll be fine, dear."

That's when I unfroze Jillian again.

She blinked. She let the principal lead her away. She had no idea what had happened.

The audience started to clap. It was sympathy clapping. Everyone felt sorry for poor Jillian.

Haha. Another great show for Slappy!

Who won the talent show? I did!

I wanted to take a bow. Too bad Jillian had carried me offstage with her!

I shook my head. "Horrible," I murmured to Maggie. "He's horrible."

"Poor Jillian," Maggie said. "I don't know her, but I feel so bad for her."

"He embarrassed her in front of everyone," I said. "And she'll never know what really happened."

I glanced at the clock on the mantel. "It's getting late," I said.

"Just a few more pages, Billy," Maggie said. She took the diary from me and flipped to near the back of the book. "It's disgusting, but I can't stop reading."

Her eyes scanned the page—and then she suddenly stopped.

"Whoa. Wait. Hold on," she murmured. "Oh wow. Billy—you're not going to *believe* this!"

12

"Read this part here," Maggie said, pointing.

I took the diary from her and raised it closer. But before I could read anything, it was swiped from my hands. "Hey—!"

I looked up to see Dad holding the book in one hand. "Sorry. Enough," he said. "I don't know why you two are so fascinated by this little book. But it's way late. Time for bed."

"But Dad—" I grabbed for the book. He swung it out of my reach.

"It will still be here tomorrow," he said. "Now come on, you two. Give me a break. It's been a tough night."

"But Dad—" I tried once more.

"And it was all your fault," he said, ignoring me. "Bringing that thing home from the dump." Dad waved a finger at us. "From now on, what is in the dump *stays* in the dump. Do you hear me?"

Maggie and I nodded but didn't say anything.

Sometimes Dad goes into long rants—especially when he's tired and stressed. And the best thing to do is just stay silent.

"I want you to keep away from the dump from now on." Dad sighed.

Maggie jumped up and gave him a hug. "Sorry we caused so much trouble."

"It won't happen again," I said. "Good night."

Maggie and I knew how to handle Dad when he was this upset. Mainly, we had to pretend to agree to do anything he wanted. Like stay away from the dump.

Dad walked off with the diary. "You can have it back tomorrow," he said. "Now go to sleep."

A few minutes later, I changed into my pajamas. Then I tiptoed across the hall to Maggie's room. I wanted to ask her what she saw in the diary. But she was already fast asleep.

Back in my room, I climbed into bed and pulled the covers to my chin. I knew it would be tough for me to fall asleep. I had too many thoughts and questions swirling around in my brain.

I kept picturing Slappy and thinking about him. How could a dummy come to life? Was he some kind of cloning experiment that went wrong?

Maybe we should have kept him. A living dummy could make us famous—and rich. Slappy could be valuable.

Or . . . maybe he *should* be buried and hidden

away under a pile of trash. Maybe we did the right thing by saving others from his evil ...

The next morning, Maggie and I searched for the diary. But we couldn't find it. Dad had already left for work. We were late. We decided we'd look for it after school.

At lunchtime, I hung out with my new friends, the guys I had played soccer with. Damien and Ramone bought hot lunches in the lunchroom— spaghetti and meatballs and salads and powdered doughnuts for dessert. I had the tuna sandwich my dad had packed for me in a brown paper bag.

The guys had been really nice to me up till then. But today they were into making jokes.

"Billy, do you get to ride in your dad's dumpster?" Damien asked. He was eating his doughnut first and had powdered sugar all around his grinning mouth.

Ramone laughed. "That would be cool. Do you get to sample the trash? Ever find anything tasty?"

They both laughed at that one.

"Did you get that T-shirt in the trash? Or does it just smell like it?"

More hilarious laughter.

I wasn't in the mood. And I knew once they started making jokes about the dump and the dumpster truck, they'd never stop.

So I decided to tell them about Slappy and about last night. I decided to show them just how cool the dump could be. And I guess I wanted to show off. I wanted to boast about this amazing thing that happened.

"My sister and I found a suitcase in the dump last night," I told them. I swiped the last section of doughnut from Damien's tray and stuffed it into my mouth before he could grab it back.

"Big whoop," Ramone said. "Who cares about a suitcase?"

"We brought it home. It had a dummy in it," I continued.

"A *what*?" Ramone asked.

"You know. A ventriloquist dummy. A big doll. Maggie and I found a slip of paper in its pocket. It said his name was Slappy, and it had these weird words."

They gazed at me while they ate their spaghetti.

"I read the words, and then a crazy thing happened," I said.

Damien swallowed. "You turned into a dummy?"

Ramone laughed. He wiped spaghetti sauce off his chin with the back of his hand.

"The dummy came to life," I said. "I know it sounds crazy. But listen to me. I'm not making it up. The dummy started insulting my dad. Then it puked up hundreds of cockroaches on our kitchen table. Then—"

49

"Whoa." Damien squeezed my hand. "Stop. When did you make this up, Billy? Is this a story you wrote for our homework?"

"No. Listen to me, guys—"

"Hey, look!" Ramone pulled a meatball off his plate. "This meatball just came to life!" He pushed it close to my face. "Say hello, Billy. Say hi to a living meatball!"

Roars of laughter.

I shoved the meatball away. "I'm being serious, guys. The dummy—"

"My backpack is *alive*!" Damien cried. He tossed his backpack in the air. "Look out! It's alive!" It crashed onto the table and knocked over Ramone's juice box.

"My whole lunch just came to life!" Ramone shouted. He burped really loud and long. "It's inside me—and it's ALIVE!"

I jumped to my feet. My face was burning, and I knew I was blushing a deep red.

How could I have been so stupid?

Only a total jerk would expect anyone to believe my story. I made a real fool of myself.

I was so eager to impress my new friends. So eager to convince them that I was cool, too.

"I can show you!" I cried. "I can prove it to you!"

"Go ahead. Prove it," Damien said. He grinned at me. "Did you and the dummy take any selfies?"

Ramone wiped his chin again. "Yeah. Show us the selfies."

I sighed. "You know I don't have a phone."

"Well, bring him to school tomorrow," Ramone said. "He's a living dummy, right? He can walk to school with you!"

They both cracked up at that one and slapped high fives.

"Look! My hand is alive! It's ALIVE!" Ramone cried. He shot his hand out and pinched my nose really hard. "I didn't do that. My living hand did!"

"Forget the whole thing," I said. I spun away and strode angrily to the lunchroom doors.

I was really mad. The guys had gone too far this time.

Know what I'm going to do? I thought. *I'm going to dig Slappy up and bring him in. When that evil dummy spews roaches on them, they'll be sorry they laughed at me. Sorry and terrified.*

13

Maggie and I hurried home to find the diary. Dad had hidden it under a pile of magazines in his room. Now that we weren't in a hurry, we found it easily.

He left us a note on the kitchen table. It read: *Don't mind the smell. The cockroaches came back. The exterminator had to spray. I'll be home early, and I'll bring dinner.*

The air felt heavy and damp in the kitchen, and the smell was horrible. "Yuck. I can feel the putrid odor on my skin!" Maggie wailed. We hurried upstairs to my room, where the air was a little better.

We dropped down on the edge of my bed. Maggie raised the diary in both hands and opened it.

"What did you want to show me last night?" I asked. "Before Dad grabbed it away?"

"Check this out." Maggie shuffled pages until she got toward the end of the book. "This is awesome. Down at the bottom. Read it."

I took the book from her and read:

Dear Diary,
I've been lucky to come alive and have had so much fun. But now, of course, my only goal is to get to The Gold. I need to find The Gold, and I know just how to do it.

I blinked. And read those words again just to make sure I had read them right. Then I turned to Maggie. "The gold?" I said. "Slappy knows about a treasure of gold?"

Maggie nodded. "That's what it sounds like. When he wrote that, he was after gold." She crinkled up her nose, the way she does when she's thinking hard. "Maybe a *lot* of gold?"

I slapped the book on my leg. "Maggie, if *we* could find the gold, then Dad wouldn't have to worry about money anymore. Just think . . ."

My mind drifted off. I pictured piles of gold coins. Then Dad's smiling face. Then I pictured . . . our house all shiny and filled with new furniture . . . a huge TV on the wall in my room . . . a new car . . .

Maggie waved a hand in front of my face. "Billy, come back. I can see you're in daydream land. Snap out of it."

She grabbed the diary from my hand and flipped through the pages, searching for where we left off.

"Does he say where the gold is?" I asked, inching closer to her. "Does he tell us where to find it?"

She elbowed me away. "Give me some room. I'm looking." She frowned.

The writing was smeared. It was hard to read. "It says something about a Coldman house," Maggie said. "What's that?"

I shrugged. "I think I heard some kids talking about it in school," I said. "Turn the page. He's *got* to tell us where the gold is."

She thumbed the page over. "Hey, we're at the last page."

I read over her shoulder:

I hate to leave you, Diary, but your pages are filled. Never fear. I will continue my brilliant thoughts in Diary Number Two.

I gasped. "Huh? Another diary?"

Maggie stared down at the page. "Another diary," she murmured. "Was it in the suitcase?"

"I don't know," I replied. "I didn't see it. We were so busy trying to stuff that evil dummy back in it . . ."

I shook my head. "It's *got* to be in that case," I said. I jumped to my feet. "Maggie, we've *got* to get that suitcase."

A few minutes later, the Dumpster Dave truck eased to the curb in front of our house. Dad parked the truck and came walking up the drive, carrying a bucket of fried chicken.

Maggie and I didn't give him a chance to get in

the house. We ran up to meet him halfway up the driveway. "Dad, we've got to talk to you," I said breathlessly.

He squinted at us. "What's wrong? Something wrong in the house?"

"No. Everything is okay," I said. "It's just—"

"We have to go back to the dump," Maggie finished my sentence for me.

Dad shifted the chicken bucket from one arm to the other. "Can we discuss this inside? I'm hungry, and this chicken smells really good."

So we waited until we were sitting around the table, and the chicken, potatoes, coleslaw, and biscuits had been piled onto our plates.

Dad finished a leg and a couple of wings. He's a tall, lanky guy, but he can put the food away. Mom always said he had a secret compartment for it. Anyway, Dad had some chicken and had downed all his mashed potatoes before he turned to us.

"Okay—so what's this about the dump? Didn't you two learn your lesson the first time?"

I hesitated. "Well . . . there's something we have to find."

Dad frowned at me. "What?"

I glanced at Maggie. She shook her head. "It's kind of a secret," I said. "We don't really want to tell you. But—"

"It's a good thing," Maggie chimed in. "Not something bad. Something we have to find."

Dad shook his head. He peeled some skin off a chicken breast and pushed it into his mouth. "I don't know why you're being so weird," he said. "But the answer is no. Definitely no. I do *not* want you going back to the dump."

"But Dad—" I started.

"I'm serious," Dad said. "Look what happened last night. That was a *disaster*." He shuddered. "All those cockroaches pouring out of that evil doll. I don't even want to think about it." He shuddered again.

"We'll be careful," Maggie said. "We promise—"

"Just forget about it," Dad said. "Whatever it is, forget about it. You stay away from the dump. If I catch you anywhere near there, you'll be grounded for a month. Do you hear me?"

We both nodded. "Okay, Dad," I said.

After dinner, Maggie and I whispered in the den. "What are we going to do?" she asked.

A smile crossed my face. "I think I have a plan."

14

My plan was simple. We had to get to the dump and pull up that suitcase. So what was the easiest way to get to the dump?

In Dad's dumpster, of course.

"This is my idea," I told Maggie. "We catch up to Dad on his Dumpster Dave route. Then hide in the dumpster as he drives to the dump. We jump out. He never sees us. We go find the suitcase. We search it. We pull out the second diary. Sneak back into the empty dumpster. And Dad drives us home without ever knowing we were there."

Simple, right?

What could go wrong?

Plenty.

After school, Maggie and I caught up to Dad's truck in front of a restaurant a few blocks away. We waited until he walked around to the back of the building. Then we hoisted ourselves over the side of the dumpster and dropped onto the trash.

But one thing we hadn't counted on was how stinky and gross it was going to be inside the dumpster when it was nearly full. There was a lot of decayed, rotting food we hadn't thought about. And we sat on squishy trash bags that truly smelled like they were loaded with rotten meat.

Even before the smell hit me, my hands wrapped around something soft and squishy. I tried to hide between two piles of old newspaper. But my hands were covered in thick yellow goo, and I slipped between two torn trash bags to the floor of the dumpster.

I heard Maggie moan a few feet away from me. "I'm . . . going . . . to be sick," she said. "There's a dead cat falling out of a bag."

I started to reply. But I heard footsteps. And then two large plastic bags, bulging with trash, came flying over the side of the dumpster. I lowered my head, and they bounced off my back.

I heard Dad groan, and then he tossed two more bags onto the pile.

A few seconds later, the truck door slammed as Dad climbed back inside. The engine started, and we slid away from the curb.

"This was your plan?" Maggie whispered. I could hear her, but I couldn't see her over the enormous trash bags.

"It isn't the way I pictured it," I said.

The truck hit a bump, and a heavy plastic bag bounced on top of me.

"I'm going to puke. Really," Maggie moaned.

"Just remember why we're here," I said.

"Because we're stupid?"

"No," I said. "Because we're going to find Slappy's second diary. Because we're going to find the gold. And we're going to surprise Dad and change our lives forever."

She didn't answer. As we bounced along the road, I tried to wipe the yellow gunk off my hands. I couldn't tell what it was—maybe slimy egg yolks. But it sure didn't want to come off.

It seemed like hours before we arrived at the dump. Maggie and I bounced and rolled and fell into the trash. The putrid odor was on my skin. I knew I'd smell gross for the rest of my life!

Maggie kept her hand over her mouth and nose. But I could see that it didn't help a bit.

Finally, we bounced over the dirt road at the dump. The truck squealed to a stop. After a few seconds, I heard a grinding sound. The truck bed began to tilt up. Soon, trash would begin tumbling out of the dumpster.

I grabbed the side of the dumpster and pulled myself up. I could see that Dad hadn't moved from behind the wheel of the truck. Keeping my head low, I gripped the dumpster side with both hands and hoisted myself out. Carefully, I lowered myself to the ground.

Maggie swung her legs over the side and dropped to the ground beside me. I pulled a piece of eggshell from her hair. Then we took off, ducking low, around the other side of the dumpster.

Had Dad seen us?

No. I could see him behind the wheel, staring straight ahead, one hand on the dumpster control. The truck bed groaned as it tilted the dumpster down toward the ocean of trash.

"Which way?" I whispered to my sister. "It all looks alike. I don't remember—"

"Over by those trees," she whispered back. "I think."

I turned toward Dad's truck. The dumpster was tilted up all the way. The trash came pouring down in an avalanche. Dad still hadn't seen us. He hadn't moved from the truck.

"This old chair looks familiar," Maggie said. "Maybe. Everything looks different in the daytime."

I started to answer. But I tripped over a half-buried wooden carton and went flying. I landed facedown in a cold puddle of muddy water. "Gaaaack." Sputtering and spitting, I pulled myself to my feet.

I wiped my face with both hands. But I couldn't get the taste of mud out of my mouth.

I turned and saw that Maggie had started to trot. She pointed. "See that heap of old clothes? I remember that," she called.

"Yes!" I remembered it, too. Maggie had piled the clothes on top of the suitcase.

We both arrived at the heap at the same time. My heart started to pound as I frantically shoved the old shirts and pants away with both hands. Then Maggie and I bent down to lift the stack of newspapers we had placed beneath the clothing.

"This is it. I know it is," I said breathlessly as we worked.

"And there it is!" Maggie cried as a corner of the suitcase came into view.

We pawed away the rest of the old newspapers and lifted the suitcase from the dirt. I set it down on its bottom and reached for the two latches.

"The diary has *got* to be in there," Maggie said. She was tugging tensely at the sides of her hair with both hands. "Hurry. Open it."

My hands were trembling. "I *am* hurrying!" I snapped.

I clicked open the two latches. Took a deep breath.

I shoved open the suitcase lid—and we both screamed.

15

Empty.

The suitcase was empty.

No diary. No Slappy. Not even a dust ball.

Totally empty.

Maggie and I stared wide-eyed into the open suitcase. We didn't speak. I could barely breathe.

Finally, she broke the silence. "Impossible," she murmured. "He was locked in."

I slammed the lid shut. I glanced all around. "Maybe he fell out. Maybe the diary fell out with him. Maybe they are around here somewhere."

I didn't really believe what I was saying. But I bent down and started pawing through the trash. Maggie circled the case, her eyes on the trash bags and broken furniture nearby.

We were still searching when it started to rain.

"Major fail," I said, shaking my head. "No diary. And no dummy."

The raindrops were light at first, but they were growing heavier, and a steady rain began to drench us. At the far edge of the trash, I saw a family of raccoons scampering toward the trees. Running for cover, I guessed.

"Back to the truck," Maggie said. The rainwater was matting her red hair to her forehead. "Hurry."

I turned—and gasped. "Oh no."

Dad's truck was moving. It had started to rumble toward the dump exit.

"He's leaving without us!" I cried.

Maggie frowned at me. "Billy—he doesn't know we're here, remember?"

"Dad! Hey—Dad!" I cupped my hands around my mouth and shouted. "Dad—wait!"

Maggie sighed. "He can't hear you over the rain."

We started to run. We both waved our hands in the air wildly and shouted: "Stop! Stop! Dad—STOP!"

My shoes slid from under me. The wet plastic trash bags were slippery, and now the wind had started to blow hard. I dropped to my knees. Pulled myself up quickly. Then slipped again.

"Dad! Hey—Dad!" Maggie jumped up and down, waving her hands over her head.

I shivered. The wind gusts were cold, and the rain swept over me, big drops running down my face.

Maggie and I huddled together, up to our knees in trash. We watched Dad's truck roll over the dirt road. The empty dumpster bounced behind it. It picked up speed as it disappeared out the exit.

Maggie swept her soaked hair back off her forehead. She shook raindrops off the shoulders of her T-shirt. Then she turned to me.

"Billy—do you have any more bright ideas?"

SLAPPY HERE, EVERYONE.

Poor Billy and Maggie. They're going to get soaked. To the bone.

I don't have to worry about that. I don't *have* any bones. Haha!

But . . . how did I get out of the suitcase? And where did I go?

That's a mystery.

I could tell you. But then it wouldn't be much of a mystery—would it?

You'd better stick with Billy and Maggie. I think they're about to find The Gold.

And that's when things get *really* interesting! Hahaha.

16

Well, I don't really want to talk about it. But the truth is, we had to walk to a gas station, use their phone to call Dad, and ask him to come pick us up. What choice did we have?

He was just a few blocks from home when he got our call. He turned the truck around and returned to the dump.

We were so smelly and soaked and disgusting, he didn't want us to get into the cab of his truck with him. And, of course, he was more than a little steamed that we had disobeyed him and sneaked our way to the dump.

But when he saw how miserable Maggie and I were, he forgot about his anger and drove home without yelling at us once. I think he held his breath the whole way so he wouldn't smell us.

When we got home, Maggie and I hurried to change into clean, dry clothes. When we came back downstairs, Dad was setting a bucket down on the floor under dripping water.

He sighed. "Our roof is like Swiss cheese . . . so many holes. Wish I had money to have it repaired."

We've GOT to find that gold, I thought.

The three of us sat down with mugs of hot chocolate and listened to the *ping ping ping* of the rainwater dripping into the metal bucket.

"Why did you sneak back to the dump?" Dad asked.

Maggie and I exchanged glances. "Uh . . . We wanted to dig up that dummy, Slappy," I confessed.

Dad squinted at me. "Why? You thought we needed more cockroaches in the house?"

"We were looking for something in his suitcase," Maggie explained.

Dad turned his gaze on her. "And what might that be?"

"We can't tell you," I said quickly. "It's a secret."

"But it's a *good* secret," Maggie added.

I twirled the hot chocolate mug between my hands. "Except we couldn't find the suitcase," I lied. I didn't want Dad to know we had failed.

"Don't go back there," Dad said. "I'm serious. When you two go to the dump, bad things seem to happen. So what's the best way to keep bad things from happening?"

"Stay away from the dump?" I answered.

He nodded.

And that was that.

67

Maggie and I got off easy. Sometimes Dad has a real temper. These days, he's in a bad mood most of the time. Mainly because he's always worried about paying the bills. And also because when it rains, our rickety old house is like living in a waterfall.

The next day was Saturday. I should have been working on my model of the universe for the science fair. I had an awesome idea for it. I was stringing up different fruits for the planets. I used oranges and lemons and apples, depending on the size of the planet. And I had a grapefruit for the bright yellow sun.

Dad said it was a waste of good fruit. I thanked him for his support. He hurried out the door to go do his Saturday trash pickup.

Maggie and her friend Laci Munroe were in the den. They were playing some kind of game on Dad's laptop. My sister and I think we should have our own laptops, especially for schoolwork. But, of course, Dad says it's not in the budget.

As I stepped into the den, I could hear tinkly music playing on the game. And the girls kept laughing as they played.

"Hey, Laci," I said. "How's kindergarten?"

"Shut up, Billy," Maggie snapped. "You're not funny."

"Yes, I am," I said.

"Funny looking," Laci muttered.

"Ooh, clever," I said. "Did you just think that up?"

Laci looks like a little blond mouse, and she has a whispery, mousy voice. She has to be the tiniest fourth grader in school. Seriously, she makes Maggie look like a giant.

I like to tease Laci because she has a good sense of humor and doesn't get hurt or angry. She plays the flute in the school jazz band. I joke that she *has* to play the flute. It's the only instrument smaller than she is! But really, she's amazing at it.

She's also an awesome gymnast. Maggie met Laci at a gymnastics class in a gym in town, and she was the first friend Maggie made when we moved here.

I stepped behind the couch and glanced at the laptop screen. "What is that?" I asked. "A *My Little Pony* game?"

"Go away, Billy," Laci said. "It's *Sims 5*. It's way too sophisticated for you."

Maggie just shook her head.

I could take a hint. They didn't want me around. I went up to my room and picked up Slappy's diary. *There has to be a way to find that gold*, I thought. *There have to be more clues in this diary.*

I dropped down onto the edge of my bed and began to thumb through it. I had to squint to make the tiny writing come into focus.

We had only skimmed through some of the pages the other night. We hadn't read everything carefully.

Maybe there's a hint we missed about where we can find Diary Number Two.

I read page after page. I found story after story about Slappy ruining people's parties, or spoiling their dinner, or biting people and hurting them.

People always tried hard to get rid of him for good. But then Slappy would reappear in a new town with a new family or a new kid. The poor victim would read out the secret words. And the dummy's evil would start all over again.

Slappy did a lot of bragging in his diary. And he wrote a lot about how great he was and how people didn't understand him:

> I just like to have a good time. I like to laugh, laugh a lot. I know how to party, Dear Diary. And I don't understand why people don't appreciate all the fun and good times I bring into the world.
>
> If I laugh at people and make rude jokes about them, does that mean I'm bad? Of course not!

Besides bragging a lot in the diary, he also complained. He complained that he didn't really have all the powers he wanted:

> Dear Diary,
> Just because I have a wooden head doesn't mean I don't have dreams. I dream that I am

all-powerful. I dream that I can summon up spirits. That I can control minds and make everyone obey me.

I know where I can get these powers, Diary. I must have them. I *must!* The powers will allow me to do whatever I want whenever I want.

And that's why I must find The Gold.

Leaning over the diary, on the edge of my bed, I read those words again. My mind began to spin. I knew this was an important clue.

Slappy wanted powers . . . powers that he didn't have. And he wrote that he knew where to find them. But in order to get the powers, he needed The Gold.

Maggie and I didn't want any powers. We just wanted the money. We just wanted to help our dad. So I kept reading.

I could hear Maggie and Laci downstairs. They were laughing about something in the *Sims* game they were playing. I shut out their laughter and studied the diary, concentrating hard.

I didn't find another clue until the very last page.

17

The ink was smeared on this page. Most of the words had been blotted out. But down near the bottom, three words stood out clearly:

The Coldman House.

Yes. I remembered that house the first time we read the diary.

I heard kids talking about it soon after we moved here. I knew it was somewhere in town. And I knew that people liked to tell scary stories about it. Like it was a haunted house or something.

"Hey, Laci—!" I shouted down the stairs.

She didn't hear me. So I ran down, taking the stairs two at a time.

The girls looked up from their game as I came bursting into the den. "Laci, have you heard of the Coldman House?" I asked.

She wrinkled her nose. "Of course. Everyone knows the Coldman House."

"Why?" I said. "What about it?"

"My grandparents lived near it," Laci said. "On the next block. But they had to move away. It was too scary to live there."

Maggie's mouth dropped open. "Why? Why was it so scary?"

"It was like a horror-movie house," Laci replied. "Seriously. Bats flying around it at night . . . strange sounds . . . weird animal howls . . . shadows moving in the windows . . . The house has been empty for years. Most everyone thinks it's definitely haunted."

Maggie shuddered. "The house . . . it's right in town?"

Laci nodded. "At the end of the bus line. The very last stop."

I waved the diary in front of me. "Well, I think we have to go there," I said. "Right away."

Maggie frowned at me. "Huh? Are you crazy?"

"I just told you it's totally creepy," Laci said. "Why on earth—"

"Because I think we will find the second diary there," I interrupted. "I think Slappy left his second diary in that house. And the second diary will tell us where The Gold is."

Laci jumped to her feet. She tossed back her blond ponytail. "Am I on the right planet?" she said. "I don't understand a word you're saying. Can you translate—"

"We're looking for a diary," Maggie told her. "I won't tell you whose diary. You won't believe me.

But we think the diary can lead us to a mess of gold."

Laci's eyes went wide. "You mean it's like a treasure hunt?"

"Yeah," I said. "A treasure hunt." I held up the diary. "I think the second book is hidden at the Coldman House. Will you two come with me?"

"I'm ready. Let's go now," Maggie said.

We both turned to Laci. She was shaking her head. "I guess I'll go. But . . . I'm warning you. This is a *big* mistake."

18

Of course, it began to rain. Whenever you pay a visit to a haunted house, there has to be pouring rain and flickering flashes of lightning in the sky. Thunder rumbled around the bus and shook the windows as we rolled toward the edge of town.

We were the only passengers. Maggie and I sat with our backs to the windows. Laci hunched between us.

The driver was an older woman with wavy white hair falling out of her bus driver's cap. She kept mumbling a song to herself and tapping a rhythm on the steering wheel as she drove. Every once in a while, I could see her glimpse us in the rearview mirror.

"Billy, what's in the bag?" Laci asked.

She pointed to the brown paper bag I held in my lap.

"It's a sandwich," I said. "My favorite. Swiss cheese and hamburger pickles."

She squinted at me. "You're bringing a sandwich to a haunted house?"

"I'm kinda hungry," I said, starting to open it.

"Why didn't you bring *us* sandwiches?" Maggie demanded. "You're going to sit there and eat that in front of us?"

"Okay, okay," I muttered. I rolled up the bag and jammed the sandwich into my pants pocket.

"Wow. It's really raining," Laci said.

"Why didn't we think of wearing our jackets?" Maggie asked. "Or bringing an umbrella?" Thunder crashed low overhead.

"You have to get soaked before you enter a creepy old mansion," I said. "That way, you can start to shiver as soon as you go inside."

"You're about as funny as a mud milkshake," Maggie said.

Laci laughed. "That's a new one."

"My brother has seen too many horror movies," Maggie told her.

"How could there be too many?" I asked.

The bus hit a bump, and we bounced in the seat. A wave of water splashed out from under the tires.

"Sorry about that!" the driver called back to us.

A few seconds later, the bus squealed to a stop. "End of the line," she called. "This is as far as I go."

I led the way to the front of the bus. She pushed a button and the door slid open. "Where you kids headed?" she asked.

"The Coldman House," I said.

She pushed back her cap and squinted at me. "You serious?"

"Yeah," I said. "It's just up the road, right?"

She nodded.

I started down the steps to the curb. Laci and Maggie followed me out into the rain.

The driver leaned toward the door. "I bring a lot of people to that house," she said. "But I never bring them back."

"What does *that* mean?" Maggie asked.

"Good luck." The driver closed the bus door. I watched her turn and wrap her hands around the wheel. The bus slowly pulled away.

I shivered as we began to walk. We ducked our heads against the rain. It was spring, but the raindrops were cold, and the gusts of wind were even colder.

Lightning crackled high above us. All three of us cried out as a tall tree, still bare from winter, tilted over the road as if it was about to fall.

Laci swung her ponytail behind her head. "Tell me again why we are doing this."

"For gold," Maggie told her. "We think there's gold."

"That's what the first diary said," I explained. "But the clues to find the gold are in the second diary."

"And who wrote the diary?" Laci asked. "How did you get it?"

"We can't tell you," Maggie answered. "If we tell you, you'll never speak to us again."

Laci squinted at her. "Seriously?"

"A dummy wrote the diary," I blurted out. "A living ventriloquist dummy."

"You're right," Laci said. "I'm never speaking to either of you again."

"It's a long story," I said. "I know you don't believe us now. But—"

I stopped because the Coldman House came into view.

The house rose like a dark tower behind a tall row of scraggly hedges. It was four stories high, the windows large and empty. A black tile roof slanted steeply down. At the top, two chimneys stood broken and crooked.

In a bright flash of lightning, the house suddenly shimmered, making it appear alive.

Laci screamed and grabbed Maggie's arm. She sucked in a deep breath. "Do we have to do this?" she asked Maggie. "Can't we call your dad and ask him to pick us up?"

Maggie shook her head. "We can't. Billy and I don't have phones."

"Well, I have a phone," Laci said. She pawed through the little bag she had strapped to her shoulder. Then she let out a groan. "I didn't bring it."

The rain started to come down harder. It sounded like a hundred drums pounding all around us, louder than the thunder.

I started to run. "Let's get inside. At least we can dry off."

I pushed through a narrow opening in the scraggly hedge. Then I trotted toward the wide front door, my shoes slipping on the tall, wet grass and weeds.

I jumped onto the front stoop with Maggie and Laci close behind me. Thunder exploded in a roar. I nearly tumbled off the stoop. I grabbed the brass door knob to brace myself.

And the front door creaked open.

We stumbled inside. A lightning flash lit up the dark walls of the entry hall. The wallpaper had big tears in it, holes where the plaster showed through. The carpet beneath our shoes was thin and ragged.

I shook off rainwater like a dog. I swept a hand back through my hair, and more water came flying off me.

"Ewwww, it smells in here," Laci said, wrinkling her nose.

"And the air is even colder than outside," Maggie complained, hugging herself.

"Think warm thoughts," I said. "That always works for me."

"You're both weird," Laci said. "I can't believe I'm really here."

Huddling close together, we made our way down the narrow entry hall. A huge living room stretched in front of us.

Dim light from the tall front windows cast the room in a blur of grays and blacks. I bumped into a low couch and quickly backed away. It was covered with swarming black insects. The walls were bare. There were big rectangles on the wallpaper where paintings must have hung.

Maggie tripped over a gap in the carpet and grabbed the mantelpiece to steady herself. I lowered my gaze—and gasped. There was a dead animal in the fireplace.

Or what was left of a dead animal.

Covered in a blanket of thick dust, it was the size of a raccoon or perhaps a medium-sized dog. It lay on its side. The fur had come off, revealing decaying gray skin. The head was just bone, a cone-shaped skeleton.

"Wow," I muttered. "I wish I could *unsee* that."

"Look. The kitchen is over here," Maggie called.

Laci and I followed her into the kitchen. I sniffed the air. "Smells like burnt toast in here," I said.

Laci sniffed, too. "Strange. No one has cooked anything in here for maybe a hundred years."

An old-fashioned refrigerator stood against the wall with its door missing. Beside it, clumps of dust were piled up in the sink. The burner grates were all missing on the stove, leaving round holes across the top.

And then we saw a large chest. It stretched wide and low across from the stove. It was a metal box, shaped like a coffin. It had a black lid on top.

"What is that?" Laci asked.

"I think it's a freezer," Maggie said. "We used to have a freezer like that when I was little."

"Think anything is inside?" I asked, studying it in the dim light from the kitchen window.

"Don't open it!" Laci cried.

"But what if the gold is hidden there?" I said.

I didn't wait for her to answer. I stepped forward and gripped the lid with both hands. My heart was suddenly pounding. A chill of fear rolled down my back.

"Billy, are you going to open it?" Maggie demanded.

"Uh . . . yeah. Sure," I said. I took a deep breath and raised the heavy lid all the way.

"Whoa!" I cried. "There's *ice* in here!"

"That's impossible," Maggie said. "There's no electricity."

The two girls stepped up beside me and peered into the freezer.

We gazed down at a huge clump of ice.

"Impossible," Maggie repeated.

And then I heard a crackling sound.

And then I saw the ice start to move.

And then . . .

And then . . .

I let out a scream.

19

My scream echoed through the empty house.

Maggie and Laci gaped wide-eyed as the ice clump broke apart. Cracking and crumpling, it shifted and shook.

I uttered another cry as the ice began to rise up from the bottom of the freezer.

I staggered back. Maggie and Laci held on to each other and slowly shrank away.

The ice rose up and started to take shape. Arms formed. Then legs. Then a head.

"It's—it's a man." I shuddered.

An ice man! Climbing up from the freezer!

I couldn't stop my legs from trembling. The horrifying creature gave off waves and waves of cold. The air turned freezing. I was suddenly shivering. My teeth were chattering. I struggled to breathe in the frigid air.

As the three of us backed away, the ice broke with a crack as loud as thunder. It fell away from the head first and shattered on the floor. And a frozen, pale white face—a face as white as snow—emerged from the icy covering.

A face of horror. Of death. Frozen eyes wide, and a toothless mouth hanging open.

Then the ice began to splinter from his tall body. His arms remained stiffly out at his sides. His frozen legs cracked as he stepped out from the freezer. His eyes ... his dead eyes ... on ME!

"I'm the Cold Man," he moaned. His voice was like the rattle of ice cubes ... a death rattle.

"I'm the Cold Man. Welcome to Coldman House."

"N-no—!" Laci stammered. She cowered in a corner with my sister, whose eyes were wide with terror.

"I've been waiting ..."

Each icy word sent a chill down my spine.

"I've been waiting for someone to let me out—"

I was shaking so hard, I could barely stand. Gasping for breath, I shut my eyes for a moment.

"Please—" I whispered to myself. "Please—when I open my eyes, let this all be a dream."

I opened my eyes.

The Cold Man lurched toward me, bringing a whoosh of frozen air with him.

"I've been waiting ..." he repeated. *"Waiting for someone to take my place!"*

He grabbed me by the shoulders. An icy grip so cold, it *burned*.

"Now it's YOUR turn!" he cried.

He gripped my shoulders with his hard, frigid fingers and dragged me to the open freezer.

20

"N-no! No—please!" A hoarse cry escaped my throat.

I struggled to pull free, but his icy hands froze my muscles. My shoes scraped the floor as he dragged me to the freezer. "Please—!" My cry came out in a desperate whisper.

The cold air froze my face and made my skin burn.

I wrapped my arms around the Cold Man's waist. I held on to him and dragged my feet, trying to slow him down.

"Leave Billy alone!" Maggie shouted.

Suddenly, she and Laci were beside me. Screaming at the icy creature. They each grabbed one of his legs and wrapped themselves around it to hold him back. Struggling to force him to stop.

And to my shock, he stopped.

My heart thudding in my chest, it took me a few seconds to realize what was happening.

The Cold Man was melting.

The heat of our bodies was causing him to thaw.

I saw a puddle of water at our feet. And I felt his waist grow slimmer as the ice warmed and dripped to the floor.

I held on . . . held on with all my strength. I pressed my chest against him as I gripped his waist tightly with both arms.

He raised his cold, pale face to the ceiling and let out an angry roar. The roar quickly became a groan. And then a gurgling whisper as he melted down.

And then he was silent. The three of us held on . . . Held on, pressing our warmth against his cold, shrinking body.

I gasped as his head broke off. With a *craaaack*, it tumbled off his shrinking shoulders. The head hit the floor and shattered into a million shards of ice.

The creature's body collapsed into the puddle on the floor. Water splashed over my shoes.

For a long time, I just stood there, breathing noisily, panting like a dog. My whole body shuddered violently. I hugged myself to stop the shaking. I stayed there, staring down at the melting pieces of ice.

Maggie's voice brought me back to life. "We're safe!" she cried. "We're safe!" She grabbed my shoulder and shook me. "Billy, are you okay? We're safe."

And then I heard someone moving in the next room.

21

"Run. Let's get *out* of here," Laci cried.

But before we could move, a man stepped into the kitchen. Not an ice man. A real person. He had a gray cap pulled down over short white hair. He wore baggy jeans, stained at the knees, and a worn plaid flannel shirt. His boots were covered in mud.

He had tiny blue eyes—like bird eyes—in a red, wrinkled face. White whiskery stubble covered his cheeks. He looked older than my grandfather. He carried a long walking stick in his right fist.

He blinked when he saw us. He swallowed and squinted at us. "Did you come to deliver the new mulch?" he asked in a quivering old-man voice.

"Uh . . . no," I stammered. "We . . . uh . . ."

"I was out back in the garden," he said, leaning on the walking stick. "I'm the gardener. Any idea how long I've been tending that garden?"

We stared at him and didn't reply.

"Going on thirty years," he said. "I'm right proud of it. It's a beautiful garden."

He motioned to the door. "The rain finally stopped. You want to bring the mulch out back?"

"Uh . . . We don't have any mulch," I told him. "We—"

"We have to go," Maggie chimed in. "We made a mistake."

"Yes, this is the wrong house," Laci added. "We are in the wrong house. Sorry."

The old man gazed at us for a long moment. His jaw worked up and down. "No problem," he said finally. "I'll take you out through the back so you can see my garden."

Before we could reply, he turned and started toward the kitchen door. His stick tapped the floor as he walked. His boots splashed right through the big puddle of water on the floor, and he didn't seem to notice.

Laci and Maggie hesitated.

"Let's follow him," I said. "He'll take us out of this house. We can come back some other time to search for the diary."

Laci shivered. "Come back here? Are you *serious*?"

I turned and led the way, following the old gardener out the kitchen door. The rain had stopped, and the sun was trying to burn through the glare of white clouds. The air still felt damp and chilly.

"This way," the old man said, tapping his stick

on the dirt path that led away from the house. Tall hedges surrounded the backyard. They glistened with raindrops from the morning rain.

"I don't think you kids have ever seen a garden like this before." He chuckled softly to himself.

Maggie stepped up close to me. "I don't see any garden," she whispered in my ear.

She was right. The yard was bare. No shrubs or plants or flowers.

"It's just weeds that haven't been cut down," Maggie whispered. "There's nothing else here."

The dirt path curved toward the side of the yard. We followed it in silence, watching for signs of a garden.

"What's up with this?" Laci whispered. "It's all just a mess. Where is the old man's garden?"

I watched him stroll along the path, tapping his stick. His head bobbed up and down as he walked. He rubbed his stubbly white beard with one hand.

"He thinks he has a garden back here," I whispered. "So weird."

Finally, the old man turned to face us. A thin smile crossed his face, wrinkling his red cheeks. "Are you ready to see the garden?" he asked.

He didn't give us a chance to answer.

He let the walking stick fall to the ground. Then he began waving his hands in front of him. He waved his hands like an orchestra conductor, moving both of them up and down to a silent rhythm.

I exchanged glances with Maggie and Laci. What did this creepy old dude think he was doing?

It didn't take long to answer that question.

As the old gardener swung his hands up and down, the dirt all around us split open. Tiny sprouts of green poked up in the holes.

"Whoa!" I cried. "This is seriously weird!"

As the gardener conducted his silent orchestra, the green sprouts rose up quickly from the ground. Swaying from side to side in the soft breeze, plants grew all around us, all over the yard. Growing taller by the second, they shot up, tilting over the dirt path.

A vine tickled my ankle, and I cried out in surprise. Another vine rose up and curled around my knee. I struggled to stay on my feet.

It was like one of those sped-up films. The gardener waved his hands faster and faster. The vines grew taller all around us. I felt too surprised and confused to run.

And in seconds, it was too late.

I tried to wrestle free. But a thick vine curled around my chest like a fat snake, and another wrapped around my waist.

I squirmed and kicked and twisted. But the strong tendrils held me tightly and tightened even more.

As I battled the growing vines, I could see Maggie and Laci struggling, too.

No use. No use.

We were prisoners.

The gardener finally lowered his hands to his sides. Then he tossed back his head and laughed.

"YOU'RE the new mulch!" he screamed. "Thanks for delivering the new mulch. It's THE THREE OF YOU!"

22

"Oh wow. Oh wow," I murmured to myself.

The vines had grown high above my head and formed a wall all around me. A tight wall that let in very little light.

A prison cell. I realized I was trapped in a cell made of thick, strong plants.

I grabbed vines with both hands and tried to tug them apart. "Let us out!" I screamed to the gardener. "Let us out!"

Maggie and Laci joined in. Our cries were muffled by the thick plant walls that held us prisoner.

Was the gardener still there?

I spun around, trying to spot an opening in the wall of plants. Yes, there were open spaces. But they were only a few inches wide.

I turned sideways and tried to edge out.

No way.

I could see Maggie trapped inside a cell of vines beside me. She was straining at the vines in front of her, struggling to pull them apart. "Billy, what are we going to do?" she cried.

Before I could answer, the rain started to come down again. It pattered loudly on the tall vines and sounded like drumming above our heads. "Maybe the rain will loosen the vines!" I cried. I had to shout to be heard over the thundering storm.

I heard Laci shout from somewhere behind me. But her words were drummed out by the roar of the rain.

I spun around in the tiny space and tried to push the vines apart again, but they still wouldn't budge.

Through a narrow opening, I saw Laci across from me. She was shouting and tearing at the vines in front of her.

"We'll never get out of here!" I heard Maggie cry. "And Dad doesn't know where we are. *No one* knows where we are!"

"Whoa." I tried ramming my body against the wall. The rain had loosened them up a bit. The plants bent a tiny bit—not enough to make room for me to escape.

I tried again. Again. Still trapped. I stopped to catch my breath and gazed out at Laci in her vine prison.

I saw her push a hand through a tiny opening. I held my breath as she stretched her arm free. Then the plants seemed to open as she poked her whole body through a narrow gap.

"I'm out!" she cried. "I'm out!"

Laci was so tiny. I always made fun of how small she was, but I'd never do that again!

Peering through a gap in the vines, I watched her run over to Maggie. The two of them began tugging together. In a few minutes, my sister slipped out, too.

"Hurry!" I shouted. "That weird gardener— he might come back!"

The rain slowed a little. Now I could hear the *drip drip drip* of rainwater falling from the trees.

My heart began to pound again as the three of us struggled to pull apart the vines that held me inside. "Go! Go! You've got it! Yes!" I cried.

I burst free and pumped both hands above my head. Both girls, their wet hair matted to their heads, had wide grins on their faces.

But there was no time to celebrate.

The gardener could come back at any time and wave his arms and build a new prison for us. Or an ice creature could attack. Or some other horrible monster that lived in this terrifying house.

"Let's go!" I cried. I turned and began to run toward the tall hedges at the back of the yard. My shoes splashed up rainwater over the weeds. I kept slipping and sliding, but I kept my eyes on the hedges.

I really want that diary, I thought. *But right now, we have to get as far away from here as we can.*

I glanced right and left, all along the dark hedges. "There has to be a gap," I said.

"This way," Laci said. She began to run along the back hedge.

The hedges formed a high wall on all three sides of the yard. The house rose up behind us. The hedges appeared to fence us in completely.

Was there a spot where Laci could slip through?

We ran all the way along the three hedge walls. No opening. No gap of any kind.

Heavy clouds rolled in again. The yard darkened, and the air grew cooler. The three of us stood in silence for a long moment.

"We have no choice," I said finally. "The only way out of here is to go back through the house."

We turned toward the house. The windows were all dark. Nothing moved inside.

Was someone waiting for us? Was someone watching us?

"I—I don't want to go back in there," Laci stammered.

Maggie turned to her. "We can't stay back here forever," she said. "It's our only way out."

"Follow me," I said.

We stopped at the kitchen door. I walked up close and tried to peer into the kitchen. But the window was covered in thick dust, and I couldn't see a thing.

"We'll run through the house," I said. "Run to the front and we won't stop. Once we're out the

95

front door and down to the street, we'll be safe."

Maggie squinted at me. "You're sure about that?"

I didn't answer. Of course, I wasn't sure. I was trying to cheer them on. Trying to encourage us all.

I grabbed the rusted door knob. I took a deep breath. "Okay. As soon as I push open the door . . . run!" My voice cracked, revealing how scared I was.

I squeezed my hand around the knob, twisted it—and pushed open the door.

I lowered my head like a running back about to score a touchdown and dove inside.

My wet shoes squeaked on the kitchen floor, and I slid out of control into the back of the long counter. Gasping for breath, I pushed away from the counter and took off again, running full speed.

The girls were right behind me. Our shoes slid and scraped and slipped as we darted into the hallway.

"Is this the right way?" Laci cried. "I don't remember this hall."

"Yes, it's right," Maggie answered breathlessly. "Keep going."

I burst out of the hall, running fast, my heart racing. I could feel the blood pulsing in my ears.

I took a wrong turn.

Into a dark library. Tall bookshelves on all four walls.

My eyes swept over the rows and rows of old, dusty books. I pointed to a doorway on the far wall. "That way!" I cried. "Hurry!"

I lurched forward—and lost my balance. I uttered a cry as I started to topple over backward. I struggled to stay on my feet. But my legs folded, and I was thrown forward, then back again.

I heard the two girls shouting out in surprise. I saw them tilting and twisting, too. It took me a few seconds to realize why I was stumbling. *The floor was rocking up and down!*

I shot my hands above my head to steady myself. The floor rose and fell beneath my shoes. It was as if the house was trying to keep us from escaping.

"I . . . I can't move!" Maggie yelled. She tumbled to the floor on her knees.

"It's like being on a ship, tossed by waves!" Laci cried.

The three of us stumbled and roared forward, then back. "Got to get to the door!" I cried. "Got to . . . move!"

I tried to lunge forward. But the floor was rising and falling too hard to get anywhere.

"Whoooa!" I stumbled. Grabbed a small table to keep from falling. Too hard. I was sliding too hard.

The table toppled over and hit the floor with a deafening *craaaash*, and I sprawled on top of it.

I let out a groan as pain roared up and down my body.

A drawer slid out of the table onto the rocking floor. "Huh?" I glimpsed something inside the drawer.

A little black book.

Could it be?

I held my breath as I reached for it.

Was it Slappy's diary?

24

As I tried to lift the book from the drawer, the floor gave one last hard toss. It sent me sliding helplessly on my stomach across the floor. "Owww!" My head banged the wall hard.

Maggie and Laci were both on their knees. "Hey—it stopped!" Maggie exclaimed.

Laci groaned. "I'm seasick! Let's get out of here while we can."

"N-no. Wait. Look!" I stammered. I scrambled to the drawer on the floor.

"I found it!" I raised the little black book in front of me. "It's the diary!"

Maggie gasped. "Huh? How do you know?"

I pushed the cover up to her face. She read the words at the bottom: *My Diary*.

"Awesome," Laci said, her eyes on the doorway in front of us. "Now let's get out of here. Before the floor goes berserk or the ceiling falls on us or something!"

"Wait," Maggie interrupted. "Let me see it.

Maybe it will tell us where the gold is." She grabbed it from my hand. She raised it to her face and began to quickly scan through the pages.

"Put it down!" Laci exclaimed. "We can't stand here reading an old diary. This house isn't safe! This house—"

Maggie had her eyes in the diary. "Slappy was here," she murmured. "He was here. In this house. And so is the gold. He says it right here."

"Okay. Okay. Hold on," I said breathlessly. "We came for the gold. Maybe we should hunt for it. But . . . where? Where should we search?"

"No need to search!" a raspy voice called from the doorway. *"I'm HERE!"*

25

I turned to the door—and gasped.

A ventriloquist dummy stood in the doorway with a grin as wide as Slappy's. A female dummy with a wild hive of curly blond hair.

She had bright blue eyes and a short snub nose. The same grinning red lips. She wore a flowered top over a short black skirt and black tights.

"No way!" I cried as she strode into the room. "No way!"

"Is she . . . alive?" Laci asked in a trembling voice just above a whisper. "Is she a puppet?"

"She's alive," Maggie answered. She took a few steps back.

My throat suddenly felt as dry as cotton. I struggled to speak. "Wh-who are you?" I croaked.

"I'm Goldie," she replied. Her voice was soft and smooth, a woman's voice. Her wooden lips clicked up and down when she spoke. "I live here," she added. "I guess I'm the one you've been looking for."

"Huh? *You?*" I blurted.

"This isn't happening," Laci muttered. She backed up to the wall, her eyes on the advancing dummy.

"It's about time that idiot Slappy sent me some new victims!" the dummy said. Her grin appeared to grow wider. "You will all serve me. I think you three will do fine—*once I break you in*! Hahaha."

"You know Slappy?" Maggie demanded.

"We have to go," Laci said. She turned her eyes to the front hall. "Seriously. It's good-bye time. This is a nightmare. A living dummy? I think I'm hallucinating!"

"Oh, don't leave," Goldie said in her smooth, soft voice. "We're going to be *very* good friends. Haha."

"Who are you?" I blurted out. "What are you doing here?"

"I *told* you," she snapped. "I'm Goldie. I live here. Slappy calls me *The Gold*. You just read that in the diary. I hope you're not too stupid to be my servants."

"Huh?" My mouth dropped open. "*You're* The Gold?"

The dummy nodded. Her blond hair bobbed on her head.

Maggie let out a sigh. Her whole body drooped. "You mean . . . there's no *real* gold?"

"*I'm* The Gold!" the dummy shrieked. "Me! Me! Me! I'm The Gold! At least, that's what

Slappy calls me. That fool likes to flatter me. Know why? Because I have powers he can only *dream* about."

"But—but—" Maggie sputtered.

"I know he wants my powers," Goldie continued. "He'll do anything to get them. Because they are *amazing*!"

The three of us stared at her. We didn't reply. Our brains were all spinning.

No gold, I thought. *There's no gold. We came here and risked our lives for nothing.*

"We have to go," Laci repeated.

"No. I'm not finished bragging," the dummy replied. "You've seen my powers. You saw what I did to you just now."

"You mean . . . the Cold Man from the freezer?" I said. "And the old gardener with the vines? That was *you*?"

She nodded. "And don't forget the floor tilting and rocking."

"You—you did all that to us?" I stammered.

"Child's play," she said. "I can do that with my beautiful eyes closed."

"That was horrible—" Maggie started.

Goldie raised a hand to silence her. "You're right. It was horrible. I apologize, dears. I wouldn't have tried to kill you if I had known you were my new servants!"

"Servants?" I cried. "No way!"

"Watch out, sonny," Goldie warned. "It's so easy for me to totally mess up your minds. You'll find out if you ever cross me."

Maggie shook her head. "No gold," she murmured. "No gold. I don't believe it."

"I'M The Gold!" Goldie screamed. "I'm The Gold. But you three can call me *Master*!"

"But Slappy—" I started.

She raised a threatening hand. "Forget about that moron. Slappy and I were made side by side by the same sorcerer. But . . . I got the brains. AND the powers." She giggled. "AND the good looks!"

I glanced quickly at the front hall. Could we reach it before she pulled one of her terrifying tricks on us?

"Don't just stand there admiring my beauty," Goldie said. "Make yourselves at home. You're going to be here for a long, long time! Hahaha."

"No, we're not," I said.

I swung my arm and motioned to the hall with the diary.

Without a word, the three of us spun away from the grinning dummy—and bolted out of the room and into the front hall. Our shoes slammed on the floorboards as we ran.

The hall was long and narrow. At the other end, we could see the front entryway and the door.

"Go! Go! Go!" I cried, waving the diary in front of me.

The girls got their legs tangled up and stumbled forward. They pushed apart and didn't stop running.

The end of the hall was only a few feet away.

"We're going to make it!" I cried breathlessly.

26

WHAAAAAM.

An explosion made my ears ring.

Like a bomb blast, a powerful burst of air sent me tumbling backward. And then I let out a scream as I felt my feet leave the floor.

Another blast of hot air sent me flying. My arms flailed. I tried to kick my feet. To lower myself. But I was helpless. Trapped in the hurricane bursts of air.

"Owwwww!" I uttered another howl as my back slammed into the wall.

It knocked the breath out of me. I struggled to breathe.

I gritted my teeth, expecting to drop to the floor. But to my surprise, I stuck there. I stuck to the wall, my back pressed tightly against the wallpaper.

I pushed my shoes against the wall and tried to force myself free. But I couldn't pry myself off.

I heard the cries of the two girls. Laci and Maggie were both pinned to the wall across from me, dangling four or five feet off the floor.

They thrashed and flailed and kicked. But it didn't take long to see there was no way to free ourselves. The three of us hung on the wall, silent now. Listening to the clumping footsteps of the dummy as she made her way toward us.

She stopped a few feet away and eyed each one of us. "Well, well," she said. "You didn't get very far, did you?" She shook her head, her curls spinning around her head. "I told you kids to *hang around*."

She laughed at her own joke.

"I think I swept you off your feet!" she exclaimed. "It's my special charm, you see." She raised both hands above her head, suddenly angry. "Don't mess around with me, kids. I have the powers, and you don't."

She stepped closer to the wall and stared up at the book in my hand. "Is that what I think it is?"

I shrugged. "I don't know."

"Hand it over," she said. She raised a hand toward me.

I swiped it away from her. "I don't think so," I said.

Her grin appeared to fade. "I *need* that book. How did you find it?"

"I don't remember," I said.

Goldie uttered a low growl. "I need it. I'm not

going to play games with you." She reached up with both hands.

I raised it higher.

"Give her the book, Billy," Maggie said. "Maybe she'll let us down from the wall."

"Listen to her," Goldie urged. "Let me have the book, and maybe I'll let you down."

"That's not good enough," I said.

"Billy, we don't need the diary anymore," Maggie said. "There's no gold. Nothing to find. Let her have it."

"She wants it too badly," I said. "I think I'll keep it."

"You're making me very angry," Goldie said. Her wooden lips clicked loudly with each word.

I opened the book and pretended to read it. "Hmmmmm. Very interesting . . ."

"I'm giving you one more chance to hand me the diary," the dummy rasped.

I continued reading.

"Billy—what are you doing?" Laci demanded in a high, trembling voice. "Give her the book. Stop fooling around."

"Let us go—now!" I told Goldie. "Let us go and I'll give you the book."

"Don't try to bargain with me. I can make it painful for you, young man," Goldie said in a low growl.

"You want the book?" I said, holding it out of her reach. "Then let us out of this house."

Her wooden lips clicked several times. She uttered an angry growl. "You asked for it."

I gripped the book in both hands. I felt it start to grow warm. The book heated up. Warmer. Then warmer. Then blazing hot as if ON FIRE!

"Owwwwwww." I let out a cry. "My hands! It's burning me! *Burning* me! My hands are on fire!"

27

I tossed the book from one hand to the other. It sizzled, hot like a burning coal.

Goldie had both hands raised, ready to catch it when I dropped it.

But I didn't drop it. I just kept flinging it from hand to hand. Sure, it burned, but there was *no way* I'd let her have it.

Not until she promised to let us go.

"Okay, okay," she said finally. She tossed her head, and her blond curls shook like Jell-O. "Okay. I can be reasonable," Goldie said. "We can make a deal."

My back ached from being pressed against the wall. And my feet were numb from hanging off the floor.

"I need that diary," Goldie said. "You can't keep it from me."

"What's your deal?" I asked.

She raised both hands toward me. "Give me the diary and I'll let you go home."

Did I believe her?

Not really.

Did I have a choice?

No. Not really.

"Let us down off the walls first, and we can talk," I said.

How did I suddenly get so brave?

Beats me.

Goldie waved her hand in the air, and the three of us slid down to the floor. I landed hard on my feet. My knees started to fold, but I caught myself and stood upright.

My feet were still numb. But I could feel the blood start to rush back down to them.

The diary was still warm in my hand. I pressed it against my chest, protecting it from Goldie.

Maggie and Laci were stretching their arms and bending their backs. "Are you really going to let us out of here?" my sister asked.

Goldie didn't answer. Instead, she charged at me. With a shrill cry, she tackled me around the waist. Bumped me back against the wall.

The diary fell from my hand.

It hit the floor and bounced.

I dove for it. But Goldie shouldered me out of the way. She pounced—and grabbed it.

Laughing, she spun away from me as I staggered off-balance, struggling to straighten up. She raised the diary in front of me and laughed some more, a horrible cackle of victory.

112

"It's *mine*!" she screamed.

She cackled again and waved the diary in the air above her head.

"Are you going to let us go home now?" Maggie asked.

Goldie stopped her celebration. She turned to the three of us. "Go home?" she said. "Did I say that? Oops. My mistake. I *meant* to say, now all three of you are doomed. Afraid I'm going to have to teach you a lesson."

A chill of fear ran down my back. "Wh-what are you going to do to us?" I stammered.

"I'm thinking . . . I'm thinking. What *should* I do to you three?" She shut her eyes. "What would be painful for you and entertaining to me?"

"*Please* let us go!" Laci cried. "*Please!*"

"You will be good servants," Goldie said, ignoring Laci's plea. "You are sharp and young. And you will learn how to obey my every whim."

"*Please—!*" Laci had tears in her eyes. Maggie slid an arm around her waist.

I eyed the front door. It was only a few feet away.

So close . . . so close.

"Yes, the front door seems very close and inviting," Goldie said, as if reading my mind. "Will I let you escape that way? I don't think so."

"We can't be your servants!" Maggie shouted. "We're just kids. We have to go to school."

The dummy tossed back her head and laughed.

"No worries," she said. "I'll teach you a lot here. Things you can't learn in school."

My sister still had her arm around Laci's waist, comforting her. Without warning, the two of them burst forward, running side by side toward the front door.

I held my breath. Could they make it?

Goldie swung two hands in the air.

The girls stumbled. Maggie twisted her body around. I could see her trying to pull her arm away from Laci.

Laci turned back. Her face was wide with horror. "We're stuck together!" she cried. "What did you *do*?"

"My arm is stuck to Laci!" Maggie wailed. "Our legs are stuck together!"

Goldie laughed her cold, throaty laugh. "You two are *very* close friends—aren't you? Hahaha!"

"Let us go!" Maggie screamed, twisting and struggling to pull her arm off Laci.

"Good friends stick together!" Goldie cried. She laughed again.

The two girls tried to pull free of one another. But Goldie's spell held them firmly.

"Haha. Stick around," Goldie said. "I've decided how I'm going to teach you three to obey me."

28

"Wh-what are you talking about?" I stammered. "You've already done *enough* to us!"

"I'm going to have a party," the dummy said. "A dinner party. And I'm going to invite my friends who live with me in this house." She sighed. "It's going to be lovely. I know my friends are *very* hungry."

"Friends?" I cried. "Who else lives in this house?"

Goldie ignored my question. "Do you know what I'm going to serve for dinner?" she asked. "YOU!"

She waved both hands.

I heard a scraping sound. A chittering whistle. Tapping on the floor, like tiny footsteps, all around us.

I let out a cry as a pack of gray rats came scuttling out, noses twitching, long tails whipping behind them.

"Nooooo," I groaned.

Maggie had managed to pull apart from Laci.

115

Both girls huddled behind me as the rats rumbled toward us.

"No—please!" Maggie cried, pressing her hands to her cheeks.

"I—I *hate* rats!" Laci exclaimed in a high, shrill gasp.

"My friends are very hungry," Goldie said. "There is so little to eat in this empty house."

The rats were definitely scrawny. Their black eyes appeared to bug out of their slender heads. Their gray fur was patchy, and open spots revealed yellow skin beneath.

The rats had been scuttling toward us on all fours. But now they stopped and stood up on their scrawny hind legs. They formed a perfect straight line, at least a dozen, maybe more.

Their mouths worked up and down, as if they were practicing eating us. Their tails swept from side to side on the floorboards behind them.

"This is crazy!" Maggie cried. "You can't do this!"

"I probably can," Goldie replied. "I don't know any reason *not* to do it! Haha."

"You don't *have* to do it," I said. "We'll be good servants. I promise."

"Yes. You don't have to teach us a lesson," Laci added. "We give up. We'll do everything you say."

Goldie's eyes moved from one of us to the next. "Do I believe you?" she said. "I don't think so. Do I look like a dummy to you?"

Standing on their hind legs, the rats began to

chitter and whistle loudly. Some of them were drooling. Others snapped their jaws, their tiny, jagged teeth clicking.

Chill after chill rolled down my back. I turned to Maggie and Laci. They were both trembling, their mouths open in fright.

"Please—" I started.

Goldie took a few steps toward us. She shook her head. "Why are you so worried?" she said. "I'm not going to let them *eat* you. I'm only going to let them *gnaw* a bit."

She waved a hand, and the rats lowered themselves to all fours and came charging toward us for their meal.

29

The hungry rats made shrill cries, almost like chirping birds. Their skinny feet skittered on the floor. They were so eager to get their meal, they slipped and tumbled as they ran to us.

Laci screamed.

Maggie grabbed my arm and squeezed it with an icy hand.

Goldie laughed and watched from the wall.

I shut my eyes and waited for the pain to start.

But then I suddenly had an idea. A weird idea. A totally *desperate* idea.

I jammed my hand into my pants pocket—and pulled out the sandwich I had packed for myself. My hands trembled as I fumbled to unwrap it.

"Here!" I shouted in a terrified, shrill voice. "Here! Here's a good treat for you!"

I raised the sandwich in front of me. I held it up so that the rats could all see it.

And then I *tossed* it. I tossed the sandwich at Goldie.

The sandwich hit her in the chest with a dull *thud*. She grabbed for it with both hands.

The rats squealed with excitement. They stopped short. Stood up. Wheeled around. And then went swooping over the floor toward the sandwich. A dozen squealing rats in a stampede of gray.

The three of us stood watching. The rats leaped onto Goldie. They scratched their way up the front of her skirt, snapping and biting. They climbed over her head, into her curls of hair.

"Stop it! Get away!" the dummy shrieked. "Get OFF me! Do you *hear* me? Get OFF!"

Goldie struggled to throw the sandwich away. But she was too late. The rats swarmed over her, attacking it.

Goldie fell to the floor on her back, and the starving rats covered her like a blanket.

"Let's go!" I screamed at Maggie and Laci.

I didn't have to say it twice.

All three of us wheeled around and lurched side by side through the short entryway. Gasping for breath, I reached the front door first. I grabbed the door handle—and flung the door open.

And all three of us screamed.

Slappy stood there, grinning in at us.

30

The dummy pushed us farther inside and stepped into the house.

"I see Goldie has some new servants!" he rasped. *"Why did it take three of you to open the door for me?"*

He didn't wait for an answer. He strode across the entryway, making his way to Goldie. She was still on her back, battling the gnawing rats.

"Goldie—I see you've made some new friends!" Slappy exclaimed. *"Funny how rats always recognize their own kind!"*

"Shut up, Slappy!" Goldie screamed. She shoved the rats off her and raised both hands in the air. Then she shouted some strange words: *"Molonu Denbar Faracuda!"*

The rats uttered a deafening squeal. Then they all rose up on their hind legs—all of them—and tumbled off Goldie. Tumbled onto their backs. And didn't move.

Goldie shook herself and pulled herself to her

feet. The sandwich was gone. And the sleeves of her top were ragged and torn, with big holes chewed out of them. Her hair fell in tangled curls over her face. She struggled to pull the strands back.

"You look like something the cat threw up," Slappy told her.

"That's a compliment coming from a loser like you!" Goldie replied. She tugged at a sleeve and it ripped off. She tossed the sleeve to the floor. "What are you doing here, Slappy? Did you come to beg me not to shove you through the wood chipper?"

She stepped over the rats and came closer to Slappy.

Slappy giggled again. *"I'm just paying a brotherly visit,"* he said.

"You're *not* my brother!" Goldie snapped. "You know what you are? You're something I might pull out from between my toes!"

Slappy shook his head. *"Tsk, tsk. Those rats put you in a bad mood. It's a good thing they didn't eat you. They'd get indigestion for sure."*

"You turn my stomach." Goldie scowled. "If I *had* a stomach. What do you want, Slappy?"

"Well . . . I'm happy I finally found The Gold. Because I've come to learn from you. You know you are the SUN, Goldie. And I am just dust in a trash heap."

"Very colorful," she sneered. "Why don't you go write poetry?"

"*I AM your brother,*" Slappy said. "*We were made side by side by the same sorcerer. But he gave you powers, Goldie. Powers you could teach me.*"

She blinked at him. "Do you have the power to shut up?"

The two dummies stood head-to-head, shouting insults at each other.

I turned and gazed at the front door. It was wide open. No one had closed it after Slappy barged in.

I held a finger up to my mouth, signaling for the girls to be as silent as possible. We turned and began to tiptoe to the door.

We were just a few steps away from freedom when Goldie shouted, "Where do you think *you're* going?"

I leaped to the doorway—and the door slammed shut in my face.

"Hey—!" I uttered a startled shout. I turned to Slappy. "Will *you* let us out? Let us go home? You don't need us here."

Slappy shook his head. "*You are our servants. I can't let you go.*"

"Huh?" Goldie cried. "*Our* servants? Are you losing it? They're MY servants. You will be, too, before we're finished here."

Maggie sighed. Laci hung her head.

I had a sudden idea. "Slappy, what if we give

you something you want?" I asked. "What if we give you something of yours that Goldie has taken?"

He tilted his head, as if thinking hard about it. *"Something of mine?"*

"Yes," I said. "What if I gave it to you? Would you let us go?"

He thought about it a while longer.

"Yes," he said finally. *"Something of mine. Something she stole from me. Yes. Maybe I'd let you go."*

Goldie didn't see the diary. I saw it in a corner on the floor. I grabbed it before she could move. "Got it!" I cried.

I turned and held it up to Slappy. "Your diary," I said. "Here it is. The second diary. The one you hid here."

Slappy leaned forward to see it better.

I raised it to his face. "This is it. We found it. Your diary."

He grabbed the diary out of my hand and studied it. Then he raised his eyes to me.

"This isn't mine," he said. *"I never started a second diary. You don't know what you're talking about, Billy. I never saw this thing before!"*

31

"You moron!" Goldie cried. "It's *my* diary! Why do you think I wanted it so badly? Why would I want Slappy's diary?" she demanded. "It's garbage!"

She made a grab for it. Slappy swung it out of her reach.

"Give it to me!" Goldie shrieked. "It's mine!"

Slappy giggled and turned his back on her. He raised Goldie's diary close to his face and quickly flipped through the pages.

"What are you doing?" Goldie screamed. "Give that to me! Right now! I'm warning you, Slappy! Give it to me *now*!"

She bumped him hard from behind. Slappy stumbled forward but kept scanning the diary.

"*There's a trick of yours I always wanted to try,*" he said. He stopped flipping through the pages. "*And here it is.*"

"Slappy, how about a snack first?" Goldie said. "Bet you could go for a big pretzel." She tapped his back three times and called out: *"Haru Maroni Melekano Gorinus!"*

Slappy made a gurgling sound. He dropped to the floor. His arms and legs slid together and folded around each other. Goldie had twisted him into the shape of a pretzel.

She tossed back her head and laughed. "Anybody got salt?" she cried.

"Go ahead and laugh," Slappy told her. His head was stuck between the tangle of his arms and legs. *"I MEMORIZED the spell, Goldie. Say good-bye to everyone. I don't need to read it. I can say it by heart now."*

Goldie moved quickly toward Slappy. "But how can you say the spell, Slappy dear, if you don't have a mouth?"

Before Slappy could reply, she reached out— and ripped off his wooden chin and bottom lip. She raised the chunk of wood and tossed it across the room.

Slappy had a wide hole where his mouth had been. His eyes rolled crazily in his head. And all he could utter in protest was, *"AAAAAHHH. AAAAAAAHHH!"*

Goldie turned to us. "Now let's see what kind of spell I can work on YOU."

I didn't hesitate. I knew Goldie would never let us out of this house alive. Slappy was our only hope.

Before Goldie could decide on a spell for us, I lurched across the room. I dove to the floor and grabbed Slappy's chin and lip.

Then I raised it above my head and shouted to Slappy. "If I put this back on you, will you let the three of us go? Will you?"

Goldie rushed at me, her hands outstretched. "Give that to me!" she screamed.

Maggie leaped in front of her and tripped her. Growling in fury, Goldie fell facedown on the floor.

I dodged past her. Grabbed Slappy's head. And shoved the chin and bottom lip back into place.

Slappy tested his mouth, clicking his lips rapidly. Then he shouted the spell he had memorized: *"Corrado Meloheeno Avay Avay Meloheeno!"*

Goldie's eyes went wide. Her mouth dropped open, and she uttered a squeak.

"Wh-what's happening?" I cried. I watched Goldie start to shrink.

"*Noooo.* Help . . . !" Goldie moaned.

It took only a few seconds. Goldie withered and sank to the floor, growing smaller and smaller. Her clothing appeared to fold into her body. Gray fur sprouted all over her.

"She's a rat!" I screamed.

Slappy had turned her into a rat. Only the blond hair remained, tiny curls that crowned the rat's head.

Slappy laughed and stared down at her. "*Her spell worked. That's a good one! Goldie always had the best spells!*" He bent over and shouted down to Goldie the rat: "*You never looked better! Hahaha!*"

As Maggie, Laci, and I stared in amazement, the blond-haired rat turned and ran, squeaking and squealing. We watched her scuttle over the floor until she disappeared into a hole in the wall.

Slappy giggled. "*Goldie has some good magic in this book. Thanks for finding her diary for me. You kids aren't as dumb as you look.*"

"So . . . can we go?" I asked. "You've got what you want."

"It's been a *horrible* day for us," Maggie said. "Please—can we go?"

"You promised—" Laci said.

Slappy returned to the diary. He bowed his

head as he read. *"Just one more trick,"* he said. *"Let me find it in here."*

"Please—" I said. "Can we—"

"Let's give it a try," Slappy said. *"It's sort of a mind-control thing."*

"Huh?" I gasped. "Mind control?"

"Yes. This could be fun." He held the book close to his face. His eyes moved from side to side as he read aloud: *"Kolonu Peeta Reeta Morano!"*

I felt a buzzing in my head. And saw a flash of bright light in front of my eyes.

We all stood there in silence for a long moment.

Then Slappy said, *"Okay. I think we're ready to go. How about it?"*

"Definitely," I said. "Can I hold the door for you, sir?"

"Take my arm, sir," Maggie said. "How can I serve you?"

"Let *me* serve you," Laci said.

"We *all* want to take good care of you, sir," I said. "We are ready to do anything you wish."

"Yes, we can't wait to serve you," Maggie said.

Slappy giggled. *"Goldie had the BEST tricks. I'm going to hold on to this diary forever!"*

"Can I carry it for you, sir?" I asked.

He shook his head. *"No. I'll keep it."*

I held the door and allowed him to step out first. "After you, sir," I said.

"We'll go to your house," Slappy said. "*I think I'm going to like it there.*" He laughed. "*Won't your dad be pleasantly surprised! He's probably running low on cockroaches. I'll see what I can do about that! Hahahaha!*"

EPILOGUE FROM SLAPPY

Haha. I *love* a story with a happy ending!

It's like a beautiful fairy tale come true, isn't it?

And so, Slappy defeated his enemy and lived happily ever after with his hardworking new servants . . .

Hey, you know I'm a nice guy. I don't ask much of my servants. Just that they shine my shoes and polish my face every morning. Hahaha.

I may start to write a new diary. It's *cruel* of me not to share every one of my thoughts with the world.

I'll also share another story with you next time, when I return with another *Goosebumps SlappyWorld* book.

Remember, this is *SlappyWorld*.

You only *scream* in it!

SLAPPYWORLD #11:
THEY CALL ME THE NIGHT HOWLER!

Read on for a preview!

How I Became a Superhero
By Mason Brady

I'm Mason Brady, and that's the title of the paper I'd like to write for Mrs. Stuckhouse, my sixth-grade teacher.

It's an exciting story, with lots of adventure and surprises. And, trust me, all kinds of danger. And I'm sure I would get an A+ or at least an A on it.

But, of course, I can't write it.

It has to remain a big, fat, superhero secret.

If I tell anyone the truth, I will lose all my powers. And then where would I be? Doomed. And my enemies would celebrate.

My identity has to remain hush-hush. Actually, I'm not even sure about my identity myself. I mean, it's very confusing. How many twelve-year-olds have to worry about a secret identity?

Okay. Let's put it this way—I'm trying to

figure out how to tell you about who I was and who I am now and what happened in between.

Well, start at the beginning, Mason.

That's how I talk to myself sometimes. It helps me untangle my thoughts.

So here goes . . .

The story starts at my favorite place on earth. The Comic Book Characters Hall of Fame Museum.

The museum is actually an old mansion located at the edge of Fargo Hills, about an hour drive from my house. It's high on a hill, surrounded by tall, bending trees that cast the entire building in dark shadow.

It has a round stone tower on one end and several chimneys sticking up on its slanting roof. I think it looks more like a castle than a house.

As Dad pulled the car into the parking lot, my heart was pounding. It was like a hip-hop beat. I could hear it bumping in my ears. That's how excited I was.

My ten-year-old sister, Stella, sat next to me in the back seat. She was pretending to be excited, too. She likes to make me nuts by copying me all the time. Stella isn't into comic books or super-heroes at all. She doesn't even know who the Avengers are. I asked her to name them and she just giggled.

Even her *looks* copy me. We're both tall. We both have short black hair and dark eyes and serious faces.

Why does she have to look like me? It's so annoying.

For the whole drive, she kept poking me and asking dumb questions.

"Mason, would you rather have the power to fly or be invisible?"

I pushed her away. "I don't want to play that game, Stella."

She grinned at me. "If you were a superhero, what color costume would you wear?"

I knew she was only asking the questions to be annoying. She didn't even wait to hear my answers. "What would your superhero name be, Mason? Would you rather be good or evil? What special power would you have?"

"The power to make you shut up?" I replied.

"Stop that, Mason!" Mom snapped. She twisted around in the passenger seat. "Stella is trying to have a conversation with you."

"No, she isn't," I said. "She's just being annoying. She isn't into comics at all."

"Well, you can teach her," Dad said.

He always takes Stella's side. She's his little princess.

"You can be her tour guide," Mom said.

I just groaned.

What can you say after a horrible idea like that?

I'm very serious about superheroes and comic book art. I draw my own comic strips, and I think I'm getting better and better.

My superhero is called Double-Header. That's because he has two heads. One head is good. The other head is evil. I think Double-Header is the first two-headed superhero in history.

I show my comic drawings to my friends at school. They all say I'm a genius. I can't tell if they're being ironic or not.

Ironic was one of our vocabulary words, and it's a good one. I use it a lot.

I showed one of my comics to Mrs. Stuckhouse, and she said, "Wonderful, wonderful." But she was in a hurry and hardly looked at it.

I gazed out the window as we pulled into the museum parking lot. "Wow!" I couldn't help but let out a cry when I spotted the tall bronze statue at the entrance. The statue of the Silver Centipede.

The Silver Centipede was the first superhero inducted into the Hall of Fame. And *The Man of 100 Legs*, as he is known, became the symbol of the museum.

One of my most awesome T-shirts has the big silvery Centipede on the front. I don't wear it very often. It's too valuable. I've tried drawing the Silver Centipede. But it's very hard. I always mess up the legs.

I leaped out of the car before Dad even shut off the engine. "YAAAY! We're HERE!" I jumped up and down. I felt like I could explode with my whole body flying off in different directions. That's how excited I was.

I trotted ahead of the others as we crossed the gravel parking lot toward the entrance. Dad hurried after me and put a hand on my shoulder. "Now I know you're excited, Mason," he said. "And I want you to have the time of your life, here. But I just want to ask one thing."

"Okay," I said. "What's that?"

"It's a very big museum. Don't wander off. Let's all stick together, okay?"

"Sure, Dad," I said.

I was being ironic.

My plan was to get away from them as fast as I could.

And, of course, that's how all the trouble started.

My head started to spin when we stepped into the very first room of the museum. The walls were covered with huge posters of the greatest comic heroes of all time.

My eyes darted from poster to poster. I didn't know where to begin.

The White Raven stood next to Harvey the Horrible. Guppy Girl, with her fins of steel, was riding a tsunami wave across a raging ocean.

The poster of The Flattener was painted by one of my favorite comic artists, Min Li. The hero's name is really Henry Punch. But he got that nickname because he leaves his enemies as flat as pancakes.

Will I ever be able to draw this well?

That's the question I asked myself as I moved slowly across the room, studying each poster.

I wondered if Min Li or any of the other artists ever gave drawing lessons.

Stella bumped me from the side. "Where is Swamp Baby?" she asked. "I love Swamp Baby."

"Go away," I said. "This is the best art ever done. Swamp Baby is for little kids."

Stella made her pouty face. "I don't care. I think Swamp Baby is cute." She bumped me again.

"Why don't you go to the baby room?" I said. "You can find all your favorites there. They have Goo Goo Girl and Captain Diaper Rash. That sounds like something you'd like."

"Be nice to your sister," Dad said. "She just wants to learn."

I gritted my teeth and growled.

Princess Stella can do no wrong.

I trotted away from Stella and led the way into the next room. It was filled with long, glass display cases. The cases had superhero costumes inside.

I hurried to the first case and lowered my face to the glass. I couldn't believe I was gazing at Lava Lad's actual costume. It looked just like a blazing red volcano was erupting on it.

"Hey, this one is funny!" Stella exclaimed. She had her face pressed against a display case, rubbing her hands all over the glass. "It's a joke, right, Mason?"

I walked up to her. "That's not a joke," I told her. "That's The Masked Monkey."

She squinted at me. "How can a stupid chimpanzee be a superhero?"

"He's not stupid," I said. "He has the wisdom of seven humans." I pushed her back. "Get your hands off the glass."

"Well, why does he wear that stupid mask?" she asked.

"It's not a stupid mask. He wears it so no one can guess his identity," I said. I let out a long sigh. I mean, how could she not know *that*?

I turned to my parents. "Stella is smearing the glass."

"Her hands are clean," Dad said. "She won't hurt anything."

Sheesh.

I had to get away from my sister. And my parents. The museum wasn't crowded. In fact, we were the only family I saw. So there was no way they'd lose me.

I waited till Stella and my parents had their backs turned, studying the blue-and-green costume of Sir Seaweed. Then I darted out of the room, through a narrow entrance at the far wall.

I found myself in a long, dimly lit hall. The walls were covered with superhero weapons. Ancient-style battle axes hung next to laser beam weapons. I hurried past silvery swords and golden bows and arrows. Flashes of lightning crackled on the ceiling over my head.

A lot of doors were closed along this hall. I didn't see anyone else back here. A wide door at the end of the hall stood partly open, pale blue light glowing behind it.

I lowered my head and took off running toward the open door. I was nearly there when I heard footsteps behind me.

I spun around.

"Oh, no."

Stella came rushing at me. "Wait up! Mason, wait up!"

I stood there with my mouth hanging open, trying to catch my breath.

She ran up to me and slapped my shoulder. "Nice try, Dude. But you lose. You're stuck with me." She giggled.

At least, she realized she was a pain.

That's kind of *ironic*.

I just shook my head and uttered a growl. I didn't say anything.

I turned and led the way through the door. It took a little while for my eyes to adjust to the dim blue light.

When I could finally focus, I saw a tall statue in the center of the room. The hero's back was turned. I could only see his long cape.

I took two steps toward the statue. Then I stopped when I heard a loud *slaaaam*.

I spun around. The door had banged shut

behind us. I blinked to make sure I was seeing right.

And then I heard a *clicccck* as the door locked.

I turned to Stella. "Hey—what's up with that?" I murmured.

About the Author

R.L. Stine says he gets to scare people all over the world. So far, his books have sold more than 400 million copies, making him one of the most popular children's authors in history. The Goosebumps series has more than 150 titles and has inspired a TV series and two motion pictures. R.L. himself is a character in the movies! He has also written the teen series Fear Street, and the Mostly Ghostly and Nightmare Room series. He is currently writing a series of graphic novels entitled Just Beyond. R.L. Stine lives in New York City with his wife, Jane, an editor and publisher. You can learn more about him at rlstine.com.

Catch the
MOST WANTED
Goosebumps® villains
UNDEAD OR ALIVE!

SPECIAL EDITIONS

The Original Bone-Chilling Series

Goosebumps®

—with Exclusive Author Interviews!

THE ORIGINAL Goosebumps BOOKS
WITH AN ALL-NEW LOOK!

CONTINUE THE FRIGHT
AT THE GOOSEBUMPS SITE
scholastic.com/goosebumps

FANS OF GOOSEBUMPS CAN:

- PLAY THE GHOULISH GAME:
  GOOSEBUMPS: SLAPPY'S DROP DEAD HOUSE

- LEARN ABOUT NEW BOOKS AND TERRIFYING CLASSICS

- TAKE A QUIZ AND LEARN WHICH TYPE OF MONSTER YOU ARE!

- LEARN ABOUT THE AUTHOR WHO STARTED IT ALL: R.L. STINE

■ SCHOLASTIC

GBWEB2019

Goosebumps SlappyWorld

THIS IS SLAPPY'S WORLD—
YOU ONLY SCREAM IN IT!

SCHOLASTIC

GBSLAPPYWORLD10